RACCOON RACKETEER

Pet Whisperer P.I.

MOLLY FITZ

© 2019, Molly Fitz.

All rights reserved. Except as permitted under the U.S. Copyright Act of 1976, no part of this publication may be reproduced, distributed or transmitted in any form or by any means, or stored in a database or retrieval system without the prior written permission of the publisher.

Editor: Jennifer Lopez (No, seriously!)

Cover & Graphics Designer: Cover Affairs

Proofreader: Tabitha Kocsis & Alice Shepherd

This is a work of fiction. Names, characters, organizations, places, events, and incidents are either products of the author's imagination or are used fictitiously. Any resemblance to actual persons, living or dead, or actual events is purely coincidental.

No part of this work may be reproduced, or stored in a retrieval system, or transmitted in any form or by any means, electronic, mechanical, photocopying, recording, or otherwise, without written permission of the publisher.

Sweet Promise Press
PO Box 72
Brighton, MI 48116

ABOUT THIS BOOK

My crazy old Nan loves making decisions on a whim. Last week, she took up flamenco dancing. This week, she's adopted a trouble-making Chihuahua named Paisley. This wouldn't be much of a problem were it not for the very crabby tabby who also lives with us.

Man, I never thought I'd miss hearing Octo-Cat's voice, but his silent protest is becoming too much to bear, especially since we just opened our new P.I. business together.

Things go from bad to worse, of course, when Nan and I discover that someone has been embezzling funds from the local animal shelter. If we can't find the culprit soon, the shelter may not be able to keep its lights on and those poor homeless pets won't have anywhere to go.

Okay, so I just need to find the thief, rescue the animals, and save the day—all while trying to find a way for Octo-Cat and Paisley to set aside their differences and work together as a team. Yeah, wish me luck…

AUTHOR'S NOTE

Hey, new reader friend!

Welcome to the crazy inner workings of my brain. I hope you'll find it a fun and exciting place to be.

If you love animals as much as I do, then I'm pretty sure you're going to enjoy the journey ahead.

Raccoon Racketeer is just one of my many brain-tickling adventures! Many more will be coming soon, so make sure you sign up for my newsletter or download my app to help you stay in the know. Doing so also unlocks adorable pictures of my own personal feline overlord, Schrödinger, deleted scenes from my books, bonus giveaways, and other cool things that are just for my inner circle of readers.

You can download my free app here:
mollymysteries.com/app

Or sign up for my newsletter here:
mollymysteries.com/subscribe

If you're ready to dive right in to more Pet Whisperer P.I., then you can even order the next books right now by clicking below:

Himalayan Hazard
Hoppy Holiday Homicide
Retriever Ransom
Lawless Litter
Legal Seagull

And make sure you've also read the books that come before **Raccoon Racketeer** in the series. They can be read in any order, but you'll enjoy yourself more if you start at the beginning!

Kitty Confidential

Terrier Transgressions
Hairless Harassment
Dog-Eared Delinquent
The Cat Caper
Chihuahua Conspiracy

And don't miss these special collections!

Pet Whisperer P.I. Books 1-3
Six Merry Little Murders

Okay, ready to talk to some animals and solve some mysteries?

Let's do this!
Molly Fitz

To anyone who wishes she could talk to her animal best friend…
Well, what's stopping you?

CHAPTER ONE

Hey, my name's Angie Russo, and I own one-half of a private investigation firm here in beautiful Blueberry Bay, Maine.

The other half belongs to my cat, Octavius—or Octo-Cat for short. It may not seem like his nickname keeps things short, but trust me on that one. Every time he tells anyone his full name, he always adds at least one new title to the end. The most recent version is Octavius Maxwell Ricardo Edmund Frederick Fulton Russo, Esq. P.I.

Like I said, it's a mouthful.

And he's kind of a handful, too.

While my spoiled tabby is undoubtedly

my best friend, he does have a way of making my life harder. For instance, he's been catnapped, ordered to court for arbitration, and even repeatedly threatened to kill our new dog.

Did I mention that all happened in the span of just one month?

But that's Octo-Cat for you.

Love him or hate him, there's no denying he's a true individual.

And even though he's just about as stubborn as they come, he does occasionally change his mind about things.

That new dog we adopted? She's a sweet rescue Chihuahua named Paisley. She liked him from the start, but it took Octo-Cat much longer to warm up to her. Now I am proud to report that the two have become close friends. In fact, one of my cat's favorite hobbies has become stalking and pouncing on his dog and then wrestling her to the ground.

Yes, his dog. That's how much the tables have turned these past few weeks.

Together, the three of us live with my grandmother, Nan. Although she's the main one who raised me, she lives in my house.

And I live in my cat's house.

Yup, Octo-Cat is a trust fund kitty, and his stipend is more than generous enough to pay the mortgage on our exquisite New England manor house.

It's a bit ridiculous, I'll be the first to admit that. But, hey, when life gives you lemonade, it's best if you drink up and enjoy!

Speaking of, I've been dating my dream guy for about seven weeks now. His name is Charles Longfellow, III, and he's my dream guy for good reason. Not only is he the sole partner at the law firm where I used to work, but he's also incredibly smart, kind, attentive, handsome—and, okay, I may as well just admit it—sexy.

Not that we've…

Anyway!

I can talk to my cat. I probably should have mentioned that earlier, seeing as it's the most unusual thing about me.

I can talk to my dog, too, and most animals now.

Long story short, I got electrocuted at a will reading, and when I regained consciousness, I heard Octo-Cat making fun of me. Once he realized I could understand him, he recruited me to solve his late owner's murder, and the rest is history.

From there, we realized two things. One, we make a really good crime-solving team, and two, we were stuck with each other for better or worse. Usually, things are better, but he still has his hissy fits on occasion—and so do I, for that matter.

And I guess that brings me to today.

Today marks the two-month mark since we first opened our P.I. outfit for business, and in that time, we've had exactly zero clients. Even my normally optimistic nan can't spin this one in a positive light.

No one wants to hire us, and I'm not sure why.

I'm well-liked in town, and it's not like people know I can actually talk to animals. They think including my cat as a partner is just a gimmick, and I prefer it that way, honestly.

But I'm starting to worry that we'll never bring any business in.

At what point do we give up on our entrepreneurial enterprise?

Octo-Cat is pretty happy sleeping in the sun most of the day, but I prefer to have more in my life. I even quit my former job as a paralegal to make sure I had enough time for all the investigative work I felt certain would fall into my lap the moment we opened for business.

Yeah, I was more than a little wrong about that one.

I need to figure out something, and fast, if I want to keep my operation afloat, but how can I trust my instincts when they were so wrong before?

Here's hoping Octo-Cat has a bright idea he'd be willing to share…

It was Wednesday morning, and I'd spent the better part of the last two days handing out flyers to any person, business, or animal who would take one. Out of desperation, I'd even visited parking lots and shoved the brightly colored papers touting my credentials under the windshield wipers of each car in the lot.

Still, not one person had called to share a case with me.

Not one.

Nan had left the house early to serve a volunteer shift picking up litter around town. We'd both agreed the animal shelter, while in need, wasn't the best place for her to share her generous heart—because we both knew she'd end up adopting almost every dog and cat in that place.

Our house was already full enough, thank you very much.

I sat in the front room of the house, sipping a can of Diet Coke. The coffee maker still scared me silly, given that the last time I'd used one I'd been electrocuted, and tea just wasn't the same without Nan to keep me company.

Paisley and Octo-Cat scampered around the house in their perpetual game of tag, and I wracked my brain for any kind of idea that would help get us some clients.

The electronic pet door buzzed, and both animals ran outside.

I smiled and watched them zigzag through the yard. Mid-autumn had hit Maine, and now most of the fire-colored leaves had fallen from the trees. While I tried my best to keep up with the raking, it wasn't easy given the fact that an enormous forest flanked my property on two sides.

Leaves blew into our yard all the time.

Like right now.

I sighed as a gust so strong I could practically see it swept through the trees and deposited at least five landscaping bags full of leaves on the front lawn. Leaves of every color carpeted the greenish-yellow grass—red, orange, yellow… turquoise?

"Mommy! Mommy!" Paisley cried from outside, and I went running. The sweet and innocent Chihuahua got upset fairly easily, but her small size also made her incredibly vulnerable. I never took any chances when it came to her safety, and neither did Nan or Octo-Cat.

One of us was always with her whenever she ventured outside.

And even though I knew Octo-Cat was out there now, I still needed to make sure nothing had happened to frighten her.

Both Paisley and Octo-Cat were waiting for me on the porch when I stepped outside. Paisley even had a turquoise piece of paper clamped within her jaws.

"What's this?" I asked, taking it from her.

"It's one of your papers, Mommy!" the little dog cried proudly.

I glanced at the bright paper in my hands and then back out to the yard where dozens, maybe even hundreds, more had mixed with the autumnal leaves.

She was right. This was my paper. In fact, it was the flyer for our P.I. firm that I had so painstakingly distributed the last couple of days. I'd handed out every single one that Nan had printed for us—I'd made sure of it.

So why had they all followed me home?

And how?

A squeaky laugh underneath the porch gave me a pretty good idea.

"Pringle!" I yelled, stomping my feet as

hard as I could to try to force the raccoon out of there.

I knew he was mad at me ever since I'd banned him from entering the house, but to sabotage my business? Really?

CHAPTER TWO

"Pringle! Show yourself!" I cried, stomping so hard the impact raced up my foot and all the way through my calf. I tried to be fair to the animals that had made themselves part of my world, to accept them for their unique selves. Most of the time that was easy…

But this particular raccoon was driving me straight in the direction of the nearest asylum.

His laughter continued from under the porch, but Pringle made no move to answer my call. I had half a mind to widen the hole he used as a doorway and climb under there myself when Octo-Cat graciously intervened.

"Angela, that's not how this is done." He paced the edge of the porch with tail and nose held high. Whatever he was about to suggest, he was obviously very proud of it.

I stopped stomping and placed a hand on my hip, widening my eyes as I waited for Octo-Cat to enlighten me.

"Paisley, stay," he said to the Chihuahua, then trotted down the stairs and approached the edge of the raccoon's nearly hidden burrow. "Sir Pringle, would you kindly give us the distinct honor of your presence?"

I heard the raccoon before I saw him. "At your service, dear Octavius."

When I peeked over the railing, I saw him making a deep bow toward my cat. For whatever reason, he idolized the tabby. At least that was his excuse for stealing so many of Octo-Cat's things. I still didn't know where his occasional fairytale knight mannerisms came from, but he clearly enjoyed this particular brand of make-believe.

Normally, I'd play along, but I was too

angry to play by the raccoon's ever-changing rules today.

"What's this?" I demanded, waving the brightly colored flyer in the air.

Pringle bared his teeth in irritation. "I'm not at your beck and call, you know."

I bared my teeth right back, just barely holding in an irritated scream. I'd never hurt a hair on his thieving head but hoped I could at least scare him into good behavior with the threat of it.

"Pray, answer the fair maiden's question," Octo-Cat intervened yet again. Oh, jeez. I'd have to block whatever medieval fantasy channel he was watching on TV when I wasn't around to supervise. Even though I realized he was trying to help, this whole thing was turning into one giant migraine.

The raccoon ran up the porch steps, climbed the railing, and plucked the paper from my hands. "That's mine," he said then tucked it under his armpit before running back to the yard and out of my reach.

I placed both my hands on my hips and

narrowed my eyes at him. "Actually, it's mine."

"Finders, keepers." The smile that crept across his face now was far worse than his earlier show of aggression.

"What? No!" I cried. Just as I'd never hurt him, I knew Pringle would never cause me physical harm. At the moment, I was feeling rather emotionally attacked, however.

"Mommy, do you want me to chase the big bad raccoon away?" Paisley wagged her tail in excitement, refusing to take her eyes off the masked thief for even a second.

"Oh, no, sweetie, you don't have to…" My words trailed away as I watched Pringle dive into the newly distributed leaves and gather up the remaining flyers.

"Actually," I said, changing my mind in an instant. "Go for it."

The little tri-color dog took off like a shot, barking at the top of her lungs. "Hey, you! Nobody messes with my mommy!"

Pringle lowered himself to all fours and shook his head. "Call off your hound. Let's discuss this like the civilized creatures I know at least one of us is."

Paisley ran a wide arc around the yard and then returned to my side. "He's still there," she pouted, then instantly brightened again. "Should I try again, Mommy?"

I smiled and bent down to pet her silky fur. "You did great. Thank you." Rising again, I marched straight over to Pringle. "Okay, let's hear it. Why did you take all my flyers?"

"They're pretty," he explained, hugging the disheveled stack to his chest. "I like pretty things."

"But they weren't here. I put them up all over town. How did you even…?"

He shrugged. "So I hitched a ride. Sometimes I like to go on adventures, too, you know? It would be nice if I didn't have to invite myself, but since you're not doing the job." He shrugged again. If I wasn't mistaken, the beginnings of tears had formed in the corners of his giant black eyes. Strange how sometimes my animal friends seemed more human than any of the people I knew.

"I'm sorry if I hurt your feelings." I squatted down to face him head on. "I didn't know you wanted to come, too."

"Of course I wanted to come!" he shouted. "I like adventures just as much as the next forest animal, you know."

I chose not to mention that distributing flyers begging for work was hardly an adventure. "Tell you what, next time we'll invite you along, too. Deal?" Or at least the next time after I'd had a chance to cool down. As it was, he'd wasted a day and a half of hard work when I'd have given him colored paper had he just asked for it.

Pringle shook his head and eyed me warily. "Not quite."

I waited, refusing to add fuel to his flaming theatrics. I got enough of this from Octo-Cat, and frankly I liked him far more than this nuisance raccoon who'd become a frenemy at best.

Pringle sighed. "I'm keeping the pretty papers."

"Why do you even need them?" I asked with a groan.

"I'm taking up origami, and these will do

very nicely." Pringle turned his nose up so high I could only see chin, then he marched straight back to his under-porch apartment.

How did he even know origami was a thing?

And how did he know enough to want to attempt it himself?

What an odd animal.

"See, Mommy! I scared him away!" Paisley sat proudly on the edge of the porch, shaking so hard with excitement that I hadn't the heart to tell her that Pringle had played us rather than other way around.

"That guy…" Octo-Cat plopped himself down beside the Chihuahua. "He's getting way too big for his britches."

I couldn't agree more, but for the moment I was done discussing the masked menace. We had too much else we could be doing with our day.

"C'mon, you two," I said with a sigh. "It looks like we need to come up with a new advertising plan."

As the three of us filed back indoors, a new determination overtook me. My P.I. business would succeed or fail based on its own merits. I would not let an egotistical raccoon with delusions of grandeur stand between me and the role I just knew I was meant to play in this world—or at least in my small corner of it.

"I know that look," Octo-Cat said with an open-mouthed smile that showed off his pointy teeth. "Nobody puts Angie in a corner."

I snorted at that one, picturing myself in the classic 80s romance opposite Patrick Swayze. Even though he used to watch only Law & Order, he'd greatly expanded his viewing habits in recent months. Largely, thanks to my nan.

And while I appreciated my cat's support, I definitely needed to start limiting his television time.

CHAPTER THREE

As it turned out, my cat wasn't the only one watching too much television these days. Normally, Nan would spend most of her mornings in the kitchen as she did the food prep for the day and whipped up treat after delectable treat for us to enjoy with our daily tea. Today, however, the kitchen sat empty, pristinely clean, and completely abandoned.

"Nan?" My voice felt disturbingly loud as it echoed through the empty manor.

When no response came, I raced to the garage to check if her little red sports car was still parked snugly inside. She often left after lunchtime to volunteer or take a community class, but she generally informed me before heading off. Besides, if she'd left the house early today, I should have seen her from my place on the front porch.

Well, her car sat waiting in the garage, right where it belonged.

So then where was my nan?

Paisley stood on her hindlegs and padded my leg with her tiny clawed feet. "I can still smell her close by. Want me to show you where she is?"

As soon as I nodded, the little dog bolted up the stairs and began scratching at the door to one of the bedrooms we didn't use.

"Nan?" I called cautiously before pushing it wide open.

Paisley raced in before me, and Octo-Cat slinked in after.

Nan, however, was still nowhere to be seen.

"Paisley, are you sure she's here?" I asked, seriously beginning to worry now.

"Oh, yes! Up there!" She ran over to the closet and began to jump and do clumsy side flips, not stopping until I looked up and noticed the open attic hatch.

I craned my neck to try to see inside. "Nan?"

She appeared in a cloud of dust. The bright silk scarf on her head featured an emoji print, and she wore cat-eye sunglasses, presumably to protect her eyes from all the floating dust motes. "Oh, hello, dear."

"What are you doing up there?" I demanded, not any less worried now that I'd found her in a potentially dangerous situation. "How did you even get up there?"

"Just sorting through some things. I started with my bedroom but wasn't quite ready to call the whole thing quits for the day just yet." She turned away and crawled out of view.

"Call what quits?" I shouted after her.

"I didn't know we had a higher place," Octo-Cat remarked, then dropped low and wiggled his butt, making an impressive leap toward the hatch.

His front paws grazed the entrance but couldn't get a grip.

"Ouch," he moaned after he fell clumsily back to the ground.

"Are you hurt?" I asked, attempting to stroke and soothe him.

He flinched and slinked away from my hand. "My poor pride," he whined. "What kind of a cat can't stick the landing? Ouch."

"Oh, Octo-friend. Can I kiss your ouchies?" the dog offered, licking her lips in anticipation.

"Insult to injury," my cat muttered.

Both animals ran out of the room, leaving me on the ground and Nan somewhere above.

"Nan?" I called again. "What are you doing up there?"

She popped into view again, laughed, and shook her head as if this should have all been obvious. "Why, Mission Marie Kondo, of course!"

"Marie Kon—Wait… Is this from that book everyone's talking about?" If memory served, there were also memes aplenty.

Nan scrunched her face up. "A book? Hmm, well, I don't know about that. It's a show on Netflix. I binged the full first season the other day. I do hope there will be a new season soon."

I knew for a fact it had been a book first but kept mum.

Her eyes lit up as she explained, "It's the new Feng Shui. Everyone's doing it. If something doesn't spark joy, then it doesn't belong in your home. Fun, right?"

"Yeah… Fun," I muttered. Already we had far more house than possessions to put in it. Sometimes I felt like we lived in a museum with all the antiques we'd inherited as part of the estate. We could do with more personal items to fill it out, not fewer.

"Well, are you coming up or am I coming down?" My grandmother tilted her head to the side in a gesture that reminded me very much of her Chihuahua sidekick. "You know what? I'll come down."

A moment later she'd scurried out of the crawl space and dropped the rest of the distance to the carpeted floor below. Her knees bent a little on impact, and I worried she'd broken something.

Racing to her side, I gently pulled her back into a standing position. "Oh my gosh! Nan! Are you okay?"

"Of course I'm okay. What do you

take me for? Some kind of invalid?" Both her knees and her voice shook, but shockingly she wasn't any worse for the wear. Not like Octo-Cat and his poor, damaged pride.

What do I take you for? A seventy-something woman, that's what! But I didn't push it since she appeared to be perfectly okay. Maybe one day I'd be in as good of shape as my grandmother, but somehow I doubted it—not when she was part Betty Crocker, part ninja.

"Do me a favor, because you know I worry," I begged. "Next time you want to go in the attic, grab me first—or at least grab a chair."

She waved my concerns away. "No need to worry. I'm done for now."

"Did you get rid of lots of stuff?" I asked, only now noticing the two large trash bags that sat to the side of the closet.

"A good chunk of it. What have you been up to this morning?"

I filled her in on the reappearing flyers and the confrontation with Pringle, ending with the most unbelievable part. "And get this? He says he needs them so he can do origami!" I exploded.

"Oh, good," Nan said with a pert nod. "I was worried he wouldn't be able to find any craft supplies."

"Wait. Are you the one who turned him on to the Japanese art of paper-folding?" Why was I even surprised?

She shrugged. "I had an old book. It wasn't sparking joy for me, but it seemed to spark joy for our raccoon friend, so I handed it right over."

"But a book? Does he know how to read?" How could he read if Octo-Cat, who'd lived much more closely with humans, couldn't?

Nan chuckled. "Well, that's a question for him, dear. Not me."

I rolled my eyes hard and let out a long, extra breathy sigh.

"No need to get snippy now," Nan scolded as she charged toward the door.

I followed her down the stairs and into the kitchen. "Sorry. I didn't mean to take it out on you. It's just I'm trying so hard to find clients for Octo-Cat's and my business, but nothing seems to be working."

"Oh, you need clients?" Nan raised an eyebrow my way while filling our tea kettle at the sink.

"Of course we do. It's been two months, and still we have zero clientele to show for our efforts." Talk about depressing.

My grandmother set the kettle on the stovetop and turned back to me with a giant grin. "Well, why didn't you say so? I happen to know someone who is in desperate need of your services."

"What?" I gasped. "And you didn't tell me?"

Nan hit me gently with a hand towel. "Calm down, you. I just found out yesterday, and I was quite busy at the time."

With her Marie Kondo-ing, right. I rearranged my features into a placating smile. Even though I loved my nan more than anyone else in this entire world, sometimes her roundabout methods could be a bit infuriating.

"Well," I said when she still hadn't said anything after a full minute. "Who is it?"

She crossed her arms over her chest and turned her face away. "Apologize first. That's twice you've snapped at me in the space of five minutes."

"I'm sorry." And I was. I loved Nan's quirkiness and wouldn't change her for the world. For all her faults, my grandmother was still my best friend and my idol.

As soon as that final syllable left my mouth, she whipped back toward me to make her big reveal. "I prefer to let you be surprised, but I'll ask your new client over for dinner tonight so she can give you all the details. I feel quite sure she'll hire you on to help her out."

"Thank you, Nan!" I sang, wrapping her in a solid hug. At the end of the day, it didn't matter that she was playing coy with the details. Nan had found a client, a real, honest-to-goodness client!

Finally, things were looking up for Octo-Cat's and my P.I. business.

CHAPTER FOUR

When the doorbell chimed a spirited rendition of the Village People's YMCA, I knew two things. My first client was on the other side of that door, and Nan had obviously been having some fun at my expense.

Nan, of course, had refused to divulge any details pertaining to the case or the client, preferring not to shade my judgment, or so she said. I personally believe she just thought it was more fun that way—well, at least for her.

So when I pulled open the door to reveal our mail lady Julie, I was completely taken by surprise. "Julie, hello! How are you today?" I asked cautiously, not quite sure whether she was the client or simply here on urgent US Postal Service business.

"I've been better, that's for sure." The normally smiling woman stood uncertainly on the porch, a giant frown marring her cherubic features. She wrung her hands and let out an enormous sigh.

"Well, invite our guest in already!" Nan called from the bottom of the staircase. I hadn't even heard her approach. I'm telling you, she's part ninja.

"Thank you, Dorothy." Julie nodded and moved to stand awkwardly in our foyer. She was one of the few people around town who knew and used Nan's God-given name rather than her preferred nickname.

"Well, I'll leave you two to discuss business in private." Nan swept away, hips swinging as she made her way toward the kitchen.

"Oh!" she cried as she twisted back to face us from across the room. "Be a dear and take the cat with you. He has a horrible habit of getting in my way lately." She paused, opened her mouth, and then shot me a giant, exaggerated wink that Julie surely couldn't have missed.

Octo-Cat growled as he hopped onto the lowest step. "Just because she can't understand me doesn't mean I don't understand her, and that was hurtful."

I wanted to comfort him but simply couldn't with Julie watching us both so closely. "Let's head up to my office," I said instead.

What had been a mere guest room when we'd moved in was now my favorite room in the entire manor. Brock Calhoun—who now went by Cal for short—had done a fantastic job converting the space into a luxury library and office, but the crowning feature was the six-foot-long window seat that overlooked the estate's back gardens. The huge vaulted ceilings and antique crystal chandelier weren't so bad either, nor were the built-in bookshelves that took up two entire walls from floor to ceiling.

"Wow," Julie whispered in reverence as she took it all in. "I bet you hardly ever leave this room."

"Not if I can help it," I said amicably,

even though that wasn't entirely true. While I definitely spent a few hours reading in my library each week, the fact I hadn't managed to book any clients to fulfill the office function of the space depressed me. Most days I found it easier to read in my bedroom rather than face my own inadequacy as a private investigator.

Well, that all changed right here, right now, and all thanks to the blessed woman before me.

"Nan says you have a case," I started once Julie had settled onto the leather fainting couch opposite my large walnut desk and swivel chair. "Catch me up."

Octo-Cat paced the perimeter of the room, trying—and failing—to act naturally. We'd have to talk about that later.

"I do." Julie glanced toward the tabby, then turned back to me and cleared her throat. "For the past couple of weeks, mailboxes on my route have been getting vandalized. And mail I know I delivered is also getting reported as never having reached its destination. I know I'm not making any mistakes, but I'm on thin ice at work. The office is blaming me and threatening to put me on administrative leave or even dock my pay to cover the cost of replacing the mailboxes."

I reached forward and touched her knee sympathetically. "That's horrible."

If I wanted to be a good investigator, I needed a good rapport with my clients just as much as I needed my sleuthing skills. Luckily, I'd always adored Julie and considered her—if not quite a friend—a well-liked acquaintance.

Even Octo-Cat appeared moved by her story. He stopped patrolling and jumped up beside her on the couch, then rubbed his head against her hand asking for pets.

"What a sweet kitty," Julie remarked, which was enough to send him skittering away just as quickly as he'd come. Nobody called him kitty and got away with it. Our guest was just lucky he wasn't in a swiping mood.

We both watched Octo-Cat settle himself in the window seat and scowl at us from across the room.

"So, you need us to find out who's taking

the mail and damaging the mailboxes so that you won't keep getting blamed for it," I summarized.

Julie nodded vigorously, then frowned. "Yes, that would be fantastic. But if you don't want to help me, I'll understand."

"Why wouldn't we want to help?" My breathing hitched as I waited for her response. The case seemed pretty open and shut, so what could be the problem?

Julie hung her head and let a lone tear fall to her lap. "I can't pay anything for your help. Ever since the kiddos started college, I've had to live paycheck to paycheck, and I'm still drowning in debt. I can't afford to lose this job, but I also can't afford to pay you to help me keep it."

"She expects us to work for free?" Octo-Cat hissed in agitation. "Thank you, next! Move along, sis."

I glared at him before turning back to Julie with a grin. "We'd be happy to help. No payment required."

Julie raised her eyes to meet mine, the hint of a smile playing at the edges of her lips. "Are you sure? I know it's asking a lot. I wouldn't have even thought to ask, but Dorothy insisted and—"

I raised my hand to cut her off. "Totally sure."

"No, no, no," Octo-Cat pouted. "What kind of hobbyist works for free? I thought we were running a legitimate operation here?"

I shook my head. Sometimes it was so hard not to talk back to him in the presence of those who didn't know about our secret connection.

"Totally sure," I said again, keeping my eyes glued to the irate tabby the whole time.

And now less than fifteen minutes after it started, my meeting with Julie came to an end. "I have to go," she said, rising to her feet and offering me her hand to shake. "Thank you so much for agreeing to help. I promise I'll find a way to repay you someday soon."

"You better!" Octo-Cat spat.

"It's no problem," I said with a smile to balance out his obvious agitation. "Our P.I. practice is just that, a practice. We're happy for the opportunity to keep our skills top-notch."

Julie sighed wistfully. "It's really sweet, you and Dorothy doing this together. I hope one day when my girls are a little further away from their teen phase, they'll want to hang out with me even half as much as you do with your nan."

I laughed. "Nan's not really a part of the firm, but we do love spending time together. I'm sure your daughters will come around soon enough."

"She's not? Then what's with all the we and us talk?"

"Oh, um, it's more like the royal we. I'm the sleuth, but I do bring in outside experts as needed." I hoped she didn't notice the way I stumbled over my words and practically tripped coming down the stairs from the shock of my mishap.

I really needed to stop including Octo-Cat when speaking with others. Even the casual we could eventually expose my secret. And as someone who uncovered secrets for a living—you know, theoretically—you'd think I'd be better at hiding them.

"The royal we, indeed," my cat sneered as he followed us down the stairs.

"Dorothy has my number," Julie said, lingering near the door. "Thank you again for your help.

"Done already?" Nan appeared, wiping her hands on the edge of her frilly pink polka dot apron.

"I'm in good hands with Angie taking on my case. Thank you for putting us together."

Nan beamed with obvious pride. "Oh, I'm so glad. Please tell me you'll stay for dinner. It's nearly ready."

"I really can't, but thank you for the invite." Julie nodded toward Nan and shook my hand a second time, then excused herself from our home.

"And stay out!" Octo-Cat called as the door latched shut behind her.

CHAPTER FIVE

"That was fast," Nan remarked a second time as I followed her into the kitchen. Even I had to admit that it seemed as if Julie couldn't wait to get out of here. Was that simply because she had other plans, or could there be another less savory reason? Gosh, I hoped she hadn't hired us to clear her name for crimes she had, in fact, committed.

No, no. I shook my head and let out a deep breath. How could I even think these things about Julie? She'd always been kind to us, always been reliable and, as best I could tell, honest.

"Looks like you have lots on your mind."

Nan pulled vegetables from the fridge and dropped them beside a clean cutting board. "Fill me in while you fix our salad," she said, returning to her place of honor at the stove.

I washed the lettuce, then put it in the spinner. Not to brag, but I'd gotten quite good at preparing our nightly veggies. Mostly because Nan didn't trust me with anything that required heat to prepare. Not after the burnt brisket fiasco of 2019.

"There's not much to tell," I said thoughtfully. "Someone's stealing mail and banging up mailboxes."

"Oh, I knew that." Nan moved toward the fridge and grabbed a stick of butter. "It's why I suggested you two to get together. Did she have anything else to say?"

I kept my focus fixed firmly on the salad. "Only that she's not able to pay. I told her that's fine, but Octo-Cat is pretty rankled about it."

"Well, of course he is. Such a crabby tabby." She turned and stuck her tongue out at Octo-Cat, who was sitting by his empty food bowl and scowling. I knew better than to feed him early, though. He'd be even more upset by the change in schedule than he'd become when he found out we wouldn't be getting paid for our first case.

"Well, excuse me for having standards," the cat said drolly. "And self-respect."

What a drama queen.

"Well, it's a good thing his trust fund is more than enough to cover our half of the mortgage and expenses."

"Indeed," Nan said, bobbing her head.

Octo-Cat let out a low growl but didn't add any words to further express his displeasure with me and the situation.

Nan and I worked in silence for a few minutes, each enjoying the peace that came with chopping, stirring, and plating up. That's when I remembered something from my past that may help with Julie's case.

"Hey," I said into the quiet kitchen. My voice seemed extra loud after the brief period of quiet. "Remember when Octo-Cat received his arbitration summons? That was delivered way late, almost too late for us to show up to the hearing. Do you think maybe one of Julie's colleagues at the post office could be to blame for what happened then and maybe also for what's happening now?"

"It's possible," Nan replied with a shrug. "But last time it was a case of a wrong mailing address and slow forward."

I chewed my lip as I considered this. I remembered it, too, but that still didn't mean there wasn't a connection now. "You know what? I'm going to grab that letter just in case. See if it sparks any memories or ideas. It may be nothing, but at least it gives us a place to start."

I raced up to the library where I kept my important papers stashed in a hanging file system in the bottom drawer of my desk. There wasn't too much I kept, but it did have a copy of Octo-Cat's trust fund paperwork, my various associate degree certificates, a copy of our mortgage, that kind of thing. Except…

Everything was gone.

I pulled the drawer completely off the track in case something had fallen behind, but not a single scrap of paper was to be found.

"Nan!" I called at the top of my lungs as

I sank the rest of the way to the ground, needing to feel something solid beneath me as panic rushed through my veins. Even though I was sitting on the hardwood floor in front of the desk, my legs still felt weak, my knees shaky. Could all my most important documents really have vanished without a trace?

My grandmother appeared a short while later. "Yes, dear?"

I twisted around to look her in the eye. "Have you been Marie Kondo-ing my things, too?"

She lifted a hand to her chest. "Of course not. I wouldn't throw your things out without your okay first. Each person needs to go through the process herself. My joy sparklers might not match your joy sparklers. In fact, they probably don't."

I lifted up the empty drawer and bit my lip to keep from crying.

"Well, now that's a pickle." She crossed the room and took the drawer from me, giving it a good firm shake.

"Oh, dear," she said when nothing fell from inside. "I'll go call Charles."

I kept sitting there even as I heard footsteps carry down the hall. Although there wasn't really anything my boyfriend could do in this situation, it still felt good knowing he'd be here soon.

While I was the best at piecing together clues and evidence, he always had a way of knowing what to do in tough situations like this.

"What's the matter with you?" Octo-Cat asked with twitching whiskers. I hadn't even noticed him enter the room.

"All of my important papers are gone," I said with a sniff.

"What is it with you and papers going missing?" he asked with a laugh, but then sobered when he noticed I was still quite upset.

"The flyers weren't my fault," I reminded him. "And neither is this."

"No," he said with a yawn. Good to see he found my turmoil to be so relaxing. When he'd finished his enormous yawn, he added, "The first set of papers were Pringle's fault. Do you think he took these, too?"

I perked up at this suggestion. "Pringle? Hmm. But he's not allowed in the house."

Octo-Cat laughed sarcastically. "Do you really think that stops him?"

"That's it." I pushed up and onto my feet, drawing strength from my newfound anger. "I'm calling animal control."

How could one little raccoon cause so much damage to my business and personal life? And why wouldn't he just leave me and my things alone?

"Oh, goodie!" Octo-Cat trilled as he trotted down the stairs behind me. "Can I be there when they come? I can't wait to see the look on his face, when—"

He stopped abruptly when a booming knock sounded on our front door. It seemed far too soon for Charles to have arrived after Nan's call, but then who…?

Nan ran out of the kitchen, wiping her hands on a tea towel that she carried with her. "Yes," she called. "Who is it?"

"It's Julie!" the mail lady answered, her voice dripping with distress. "Can I come in?"

CHAPTER SIX

Julie, Nan, and I stood in the foyer with Paisley at our heels and Octo-Cat watching from what he deemed a safe distance part-way up the stairs.

"What's wrong?" I asked as Julie's shoulders shook from crying.

Nan put an arm around the mail lady's shoulders and offered a tissue she'd pulled from her front pocket.

"I was hardly here for ten minutes," Julie reminded us. "And yet someone ransacked my truck. I didn't notice until I'd already driven all the way home, and I still can't believe it."

"What's missing?" I asked, fearing what her answer might be.

"Some packages that I was unable to deliver since I had no one to sign for them." Her expression grew dark, angry. "I'm already in just about as much trouble as I can get at work. What I'm really upset about is that my lucky angel was taken, too."

"Doesn't sound very lucky anymore," Octo-Cat quipped, then laughed at his own joke, his striped, furry head tilting from side to side.

"Your lucky angel?" I asked, dread rising in my chest. I could always print more flyers or order new copies of my paperwork. A lucky angel sounded like it might be irreplaceable.

"Oh, it's not an expensive thing, but it was real special to me. It was the first Mother's Day gift my girls ever bought for me with their own money. It's mostly glass with a bit of gold-like plating along the edges. I keep it in the glove compartment since it's fragile. That way, it's always close enough to keep me company as I go about my day."

"How'd you find out it was missing?" I

asked, resisting the urge to start biting at my fingernails from the mounting anxiety.

Julie got a far-off look in her eyes and she swayed slightly from side to side as if in a dream. "My youngest called to update me on college life. That's why I was in such a rush to say goodbye after our visit, because I knew she'd be calling to check in after the shift at her part-time job ended tonight. I like to hold onto the angel while I talk with either of my girls. It's the next best thing to being able to hug them in my arms."

"But when you went to get it, it wasn't there," I finished for her with a sigh.

She nodded and pointed at me. "Exactly."

"But you knew it was still in your truck before you came to visit us?" This whole thing was giving me a headache. It had to have been Pringle, which meant his kleptomania had reached alarmingly dangerous heights.

"Of course, it was!" Julie exploded. Suddenly, it didn't feel as if we were allies trying to solve this thing together. "Like I said, it's my lucky charm, and I figured I'd need a good bit of luck heading into our meeting, hoping you'd agree to help me for free and all." She dropped her voice to a husky whisper and glanced hesitantly toward Nan. "D-d-d-did you take my angel, Dorothy?"

Oh, no. It was one thing to blame me, but to even think Nan could... Impossible! Of course, I was quick to defend my grandmother. "No way! You and I both know she didn't, but I have a pretty good idea who did."

"Let me guess..." Octo-Cat descended the steps slowly and plopped himself between Julie and me. "A certain, up-to-no-good-ever raccoon?"

Paisley began to bark furiously at this. "Big, bad raccoon!" she cried. "He hurt Mommy's friend!"

Julie glanced nervously toward the upset little dog and stepped closer to the door.

"Shh, it's okay, baby," Nan said, lifting Paisley into her arms and giving her a big, wet kiss.

I kept my attention focused squarely on Julie as I explained, "There's a raccoon with sticky fingers that lives under our front porch. And, well, I wouldn't be surprised one bit if he's the one who snuck into your truck and stole your angel. The packages, too."

"Angie's also had some things go missing recently," Nan explained, and we've already caught him red-handed once.

Julie's head whipped back at this news as if she'd just received a blow right to her face. "A raccoon is taking your things? You know this for sure, and yet you haven't exterminated him yet?"

How could I explain that killing the raccoon would be akin to murdering a human in my book? No matter how much he got on my nerves, I would never hurt him to make my life run a little smoother.

"My dear Angie has a soft heart," Nan explained with a sad smile.

"Can you get it back for me?" Julie asked with another sniffle. I had no idea whether this newest round of tears were caused by sorrow or by hope—or perhaps both at the same time. "Can you get my angel back?"

"Of course, we can," I said, shooting a

worrying glance Nan's way. If I was going to recover stolen property from a raccoon burrow, I'd need a bit of privacy to do it.

"Dinner's just about ready," my grandmother said right on cue. "While Angie is out dealing with the raccoon, I'll need someone to stay here and eat it with me. C'mon, dear." She guided Julie toward the dining room before anyone could argue.

I marched out the door with the animals in close pursuit. And even though I wanted to scream at the top of my lungs, I had to play it cool or risk Julie overhearing.

"I'll get him, Mommy!" Paisley volunteered, and before I could stop her she ran into the raccoon's lair beneath the porch.

"Paisley, no!" I hissed, worry beating its ugly wings within me. "Get back here!"

Pringle was about five times her size and could really hurt her if he felt threatened by her unexpected entry into his home.

"Well, this could all go terribly, terribly wrong," Octo-Cat said with a sigh. "That's dogs for you, though. Always doing. Never thinking." Yes, Paisley had become his closest friend in recent months—and, no, he hadn't waivered one bit in his prejudice toward dogs. Contradictions were okay in his book, as long as he was the one making them.

Tires crunched in the distance, and I glanced up just in time to see Charles's car pulling up our long driveway.

He parked right in front of the porch. "Nan told me you're having a little raccoon problem," he said as he moved around to the trunk of his car and popped the lid.

"More like a big raccoon problem," I mumbled.

Charles grabbed a pair of shovels and a flashlight, then slammed the trunk closed again. "Well then, let's get to work. Shall we?"

CHAPTER SEVEN

Charles and I approached the slim, jagged hole that led into Pringle's under-porch apartment, shovels in hand. Octo-Cat stayed on the porch, preferring not to get directly involved if he could avoid it. Paisley, of course, had already charged bravely ahead against my wishes.

"Pringle," I whisper-yelled at the hole, praying he was in a good enough mood to spare my poor overeager Chihuahua warrior. "Get out here!"

A little head with shining eyes poked out through the overturned grass and dirt—not Pringle's, but Paisley's. Oh, thank goodness!

"Hi, Mommy," she said with a giant,

excited shiver. "The raccoon isn't home, but he sure has a lot of stuff under there!"

More than anything, I was happy to see Paisley had survived her foolish venture without so much as a scratch on her tiny head, but I was also happy about the intel she'd gotten for us.

"I guess that works in our favor," I said. "It will be easier to get in there and get what we need without raccoon interference." Glancing up at Charles, I backtracked a little and explained, "Pringle's not home."

He chuckled good-naturedly. "Yup, I got that from context. I'm getting really good at understanding your one-sided conversations, you know. I've had lots and lots of practice."

Heat rushed to my cheeks, followed closely by Charles's lips as he pressed them against my skin. Instantly, I felt better, more in control of the situation. What can I say? He just had that kind of effect on me.

I hummed a satisfied beat. "How did I get so lucky to land the best boyfriend in all of Blueberry Bay?" I asked, turning to press my mouth directly to his.

"Only Blueberry Bay?" Charles asked as

he playfully twisted a strand of my hair around his index finger, then bopped my nose.

"Okay, then how about the whole state of Maine?" I suggested with a wink.

"How about eww, gross, not in front of the cat?" Octo-Cat groused, jumping off the porch and charging over to stand between us. "This is the reason I call him UpChuck. Every time he's around, the two of you make me want to vomit."

Actually, my cat had begun referring to my boyfriend as UpChuck long before we'd started dating, but now wasn't the time to argue over the timeline. We had a raccoon hideout to raid.

I raised my shovel and smiled awkwardly at my companions. "Ready?"

Charles answered by stabbing his shovel down into the ground and lifting out a giant heap of dirt. "Oh, yeah."

"This is almost as disgusting as what you two were doing before," Octo-Cat growled, returning to the porch. He loved exploring the outdoors but hated getting dirty. Sure enough, the sight of the disturbed dirt was enough to have him whipping out his sandpaper tongue and getting to work.

"How can I help, Mommy?" Paisley asked, shifting her weight back and forth between her two front paws in a merry little dance. Unlike the cat, she loved any and every chance to get dirty. On more than one occasion, I'd found her in our laundry room rolling around in the dirty clothes pile with an expression of absolutely unfettered joy.

"Stay out of the way for right now, because I don't want you to get hurt while we're digging."

Paisley's face fell for an instant. It seemed she was the only one who didn't understand how small and vulnerable she could be when danger struck—and even when it didn't. Even though I wanted to keep her safe, I knew better than to completely exclude her from our mission.

"Once we're done digging, you can help bring things out," I offered, making my voice high and hyper. "Deal?"

"Deal," she barked and ran up the porch steps. She had a hard time running in a straight line since her tail was wagging so furiously. Still, she made it to her kitty bestie's side, tail still wagging a staccato against the porch floorboards.

Turning my attention back to the matter at hand, I realized the pile of dirt beside Charles had grown by several shovelfuls now and I hadn't even broken earth yet. I raised my shovel again, ready to dig in, when Charles stopped me with a sharp command.

"Grab the flashlight and see what you can make out under there," he said, lifting yet another pile of dirt out of the way.

I searched the yard until I spotted the flashlight lying in a nearby patch of grass. Grabbing it with both hands, I switched it on. Twilight had already begun to set in. Within half an hour, the sky would be completely dark. We needed to hurry. I had no idea when Pringle would be back, but I knew he had the benefit of night vision plus knowledge of the terrain. And while Octo-Cat could see in the dark, he wasn't exactly the most hands-on when it came to tonight's task.

I approached the widened hole carefully so as not to be greeted by a shovelful of dirt to the face and dropped to my hands and knees, lowering myself all the way to my stomach. With the flashlight's help, I could now see most of the space beneath the porch for the first time ever.

"Oh my gosh," I squealed, forgetting to keep my voice low so as not to be overheard by Julie inside. "It's like a dragon's lair under there. No wonder he thinks of himself as some kind of fairytale knight."

I just could not get over how much the raccoon had managed to stash in such a confined space. Everywhere I looked, slim boxes, messy stacks of paper, bits of trash, foil, and assorted odds and ends from inside our house crowded the edges of the lair. I spotted a throw pillow that had been missing for weeks. Even one of Octo-Cat's prized teacups. Oh, he was going to be livid over that one.

"Do you see my angel?" Julie asked from behind me. I hadn't even heard her come outside, but now that she was here, I needed to be extra careful with how I proceeded.

Sweeping my light around the hidey hole a second time, I tried to focus on anything that caught and played with the light. I'd just about given up on finding it without having to physically get into the space when a little sparkle of shining gold caught my eye.

"Yes! Yes, I see it!" I cried excitedly. The sooner we could return Julie's stolen treasure, the sooner we could get her out of here and the better we could protect my secret. I reached into the hole as far as I could but came up at least a foot short.

"Paisley," I called. "Can you help Mommy get the angel?"

The Chihuahua, always eager to please, ran over with a joyous bark, then dived right back into the hole.

I continued to stretch my arm toward the angel and pointed. "Right there. Bring it to Mommy!"

Paisley darted toward the angel and clutched it in her mouth. Unlike Octo-Cat, she didn't mind when I talked to her the way humans normally talked to animals. She was just so happy to be a part of Nan's and my life, she never really questioned anything we did or how we chose to do it.

"Good dog!" I gushed as she made her way back to me. "Good dog!"

Charles helped me back to my feet, then Paisley emerged with the prized possession still held securely between her jaws.

"Oh, that's it," Julie said with yet another sniffle as she bent down to accept the trinket from Paisley. "That's my angel. Thank you. Thank you so much!"

"Sorry about that. The good news is that a little polish should have it as good as new," I said, hoping this observation would prove to be true.

"Clearly we need to do something about that raccoon," Nan added with a heavy sigh as she shook her head.

We stood in silence for a few moments, until…

A chittering yowl hurtled through the air, an angry raccoon following close behind it. "My home! What have you done to my home?" Pringle yelled, lifting both hands to his head and looking as if he were trying to push his brains back in through his ears.

"Get back!" Julie cried, keeping her eyes

on Pringle as she backed slowly toward her truck. "That thing could have rabies."

"Rabies?" Pringle fell to all fours and ambled after Julie. "That's speciesist, and I don't appreciate it... Hey, wait, that's mine!"

"Stop!" I shouted just as Pringle raised himself to his hindlegs again and was making ready to swipe the angel straight out of Julie's hands.

Everyone turned toward me, waiting to see what my big plan was. Um, I didn't have one. Not yet, anyway.

"Julie, you should go. I'll call you later to check in on your case. First I need to deal with our raccoon friend here," I muttered.

I just hoped my use of the word friend might soften Pringle to what was coming next.

CHAPTER EIGHT

We all watched in silence as Julie hightailed it out of there. I couldn't really blame her for wanting to escape the disaster unfolding in my front yard. The poor thing had been framed for mail theft and property damage, had something special stolen right out of her vehicle, and then, to top it all off, she'd been chased after by an angry raccoon.

Unfortunately, what was a horror show for most people was just another day in my zany, critter-filled life—and this one wasn't even close to over yet.

Pringle turned on me, fury filling his

dark eyes. "Hey, lady. You've got some serious explaining to do."

"Me?" I screeched. Finally, I could be as loud as I wanted without fearing discovery. "You're the one who stole my flyers, Julie's angel, and apparently half the neighborhood, too."

Pringle clicked his tongue and stared down his nose at me. "Haven't we moved past the flyers?"

"No, we have not moved past the flyers! Why do you keep taking everything that isn't nailed down?" A sudden shocking thought occurred to me, sending a shiver straight through my body. "Are we going to have to start nailing everything down?"

Pringle flashed a devilish grin my way. "You can try, but I know how to use a hammer."

My goodness! He knew how to read, how to use a hammer, how to break his way into a car. Was there anything this crazy creature couldn't do?

"Stop messing with my life," I said between clenched teeth.

He took a staggering step back. "Me?

Mess with your life? I'll have you know that I was here first, Missy."

"Um, Angie dear?" Nan broke in at a good moment considering I had no idea how I was going to respond to his latest jab. "Do the two of you need some privacy?"

"No. Of course not," I said, shaking my head with a huff.

"Actually, yes," Pringle countered. "If we're going to have it out, it's best that there aren't any witnesses."

I gulped hard, blinking in disbelief. "Did you just threaten me?"

He shrugged nonchalantly. "Maybe I did. The question is what are you going to do about it?"

Paisley jumped into the fray, angrily kicking her feet up behind her in a move that resembled chicken scratch. "Nobody hurts my mommy!"

"Relax, half-pint. I'm not going to hurt her," he told the dog. "Although I should, considering what she's done to my beautiful home. It's in ruins!"

"Give me a break. You literally live in a hole in the ground," Octo-Cat mumbled.

Pringle sank back onto his haunches and shook his head. "That cut me deep, Octavius. Real deep."

"Um, maybe you guys should go," I told Nan, seeing as we were getting nowhere with all the intrusions to our conversation. Pringle and I needed to have this out without my cat mocking him or my dog threatening him, and I just needed to be done with this whole migraine-inducing ordeal. "Take Paisley and Octo-Cat, too."

Charles squeezed my shoulder before reaching down to scoop up the agitated Chihuahua. "Let's go, guys," he said.

"This isn't over!" Paisley shouted in her adorably squeaky and very non-scary voice. "It's not even close to over!"

"Shh, baby girl. Shh," Nan cooed.

And together the two humans and two animals marched back into the house, the animals less than enthusiastic about leaving me behind to deal with the raccoon drama on my own.

"Why are you stealing things?" I demanded with my arms crossed over my chest once Pringle and I were alone in the yard again.

"I'm not stealing." He stopped to roll his eyes as if talking to the biggest moron on the planet—I most definitely did not appreciate that implication. "Look, it's a simple case of manifest destiny. Right? I'm not stealing things. I'm claiming them in the name of Pringle."

"How is that different?" Did he really just trot out one of the terms I'd learned in middle school U.S. History and then use it to justify his crimes? This was going to be a long night, and I could feel it getting even longer.

"Look, I'm no dummy. I've read your human history books. I know all about how this country was founded. Well done, I might add. Those guys decided they wanted more land, so they took it. I decided I wanted more treasures, so I took them. So what?"

"This is not the age of exploration," I countered in disbelief. "And it's not okay to take things without permission. It wasn't really okay then, either, but hindsight and all that."

"Well, sorrrrrry. I didn't realize the rules changed depending on who they applied to."

The worst part was how Pringle absolutely nailed his argument against humanity. Any argument I made would sound unintelligent by comparison, and I didn't want to resort to being a bully.

Luckily, Pringle kept right on going. "If you're going to be such a wet blanket about it, then take all your stupid human trash back. I didn't find what I was looking for anyway."

Well, this was new information.

"What were you looking for?" I asked breathlessly, more curious than annoyed now.

The raccoon lifted both hands into the darkening sky and shook them in a bang-on display of jazz hands. "Secrets," he whispered dramatically.

That took me by surprise. "What do you mean secrets?"

"Exactly what I said. I like reading and watching TV as much as the next guy, but it's all fake, made-up stuff. The drama is far more interesting when it's real. Don't you think?"

I swallowed hard, then sputtered, "Um, what do you mean?"

"I'm talking secrets, honey." Pringle raised one eyebrow and shook his head. "Have you really forgotten already?"

I was almost afraid to ask the next question, but I couldn't keep it in. "What secrets do you have under there?"

"Most of them are pretty tame. The MacIntyres are behind on their utility bills. A kid a few blocks over has an arraignment next week on shoplifting charges. Mild stuff. Well, most of the time, anyway."

And just like that, all the remaining pieces clicked into place. "So, it was you taking the mail?"

"Of course it was me!" He threw both hands up in the air as if he couldn't even deal with my slow human brain anymore.

But I still had more questions. "Why did you vandalize the mailboxes?"

He shrugged. "Seemed like a good idea at the time. Aren't you going to ask about the big secret I have?"

I shivered. Yes, I was curious, but this

had to end somewhere, and I worried that by taking too much of a visible interest, Pringle would assume his bad behavior was justified. "I don't really like gossip, so no. Thank you, though."

"That's too bad," the raccoon said, a sinister smile spreading from cheek to furry cheek. "If it were me, I'd want to know."

"Know what?" I asked, hating myself for playing right into his sticky little hands.

He dropped to all fours and closed the distance between us. Placing one hand on my shoe, he stared up at me with wide, intelligent eyes. "Know that the one person I trusted the most in this world has been lying to me my whole life."

No. No way. It couldn't be.

Why was I even listening to this? Clearly, Pringle was just trying to stir up trouble, and yet…

"Nan?" I asked, my voice shaking.

Pringle nodded, a solemn expression overtaking his dark face. "Guess it's not a secret anymore."

CHAPTER NINE

According to the raccoon that lived under my porch, my nan had some kind of deep, dark secret that would change everything. We'd already established that Pringle was a thief. Could he be a liar, too?

I should have turned away and refused to hear any more, but I just couldn't help but wonder... Might the raccoon be telling the truth?

Pringle placed a hand on my leg and gave me a short series of pats. "There, there, princess. I can see you're taking this hard. I can also see that you haven't decided whether or not you believe me, so let me do you a solid."

He turned away ruefully and slipped under the porch, emerging mere seconds later with an aged envelope gripped in his hand. He lifted it toward me in offering. "Be careful with this. I don't want you getting any dirty human fingerprints on it or otherwise contaminating the best secret I've ever collected."

My hands shook as I accepted the thin letter. It had already been covered in actual dirt from its time within the raccoon's lair, so I didn't see how my touching it could make things any worse. The envelope had been torn clear across the top, and there was a single sheet of cream-colored paper folded and placed inside.

Dorothy Loretta Lee was written in a tight, controlled script. The top corner didn't have a sender's name, only an address somewhere in Georgia. Seeing it firsthand, I had no doubt the letter was authentic.

"Read it," the raccoon urged, watching me with a shiny, probing gaze.

"Where did you get this?" I asked, still not ready, doubting I'd ever be ready.

"From your nan's things," he said with a

slow nod. "It was a couple weeks ago. I noticed her going up into the attic, and then I remembered that I have a private entrance into that place, so I climbed through the hole in the roof, and—"

"Wait. There's a hole in my roof?"

"Not the point of my story." He paused, presumably to make sure I had no other questions or arguments before he continued. "Anyway, I climbed through the hole in the roof, but I couldn't find anything good. So I watched and waited. Eventually she went back, and that's when I saw she had a special hiding place tucked into the wall. There was this wooden border between the floor and the wall."

"Baseboard trim?" I suggested gently. Why was I getting caught up in the details?

"Sure. Whatever. Point is if you kick it, it falls out, and behind it, there's a hole. I found a lot of pretty green papers there, too."

"Green papers?" I gasped. Could he mean…? "Would you show them to me?"

"Sure thing, babe." Pringle went back under the porch and was gone for a little longer this time. As tempted as I was to read the letter, I still couldn't bring myself to face whatever truths it would reveal. Would I still be able to look at my beloved nan the same way once I knew?

The raccoon returned with a giant wad of bundled bills in his hands. One-hundred-dollar bills.

"Pretty, right?" he asked with a smile. "They're not exactly the right shape, but I thought they might make nice paper cranes once I get going with my origami."

"Give me that," I said at the same time I grabbed the currency from his paws. "This came from Nan's hiding place in the attic?"

"Yeah, it was with the letter and some other papers. They were boring, though." He tilted his head to the side in thought and then amended his previous statement with, "Well, all except one."

"Can I see them?" I asked, just short of begging. Anything to stall a bit longer.

Pringle shook his head and clicked his tongue. "How about you read the letter, eh? I'm going to need it back, so just get on with it already."

He was right. I couldn't stall any longer. Reaching into the envelope, I pulled out the antique letter at last and attempted to smooth the wrinkles before lifting it toward a beam of light from the porch.

"Careful with that. It's important to me," Pringle hissed, but I had already tuned him out and lost myself in the words that waited for me on that page.

Dear Dorothy,

Dorothy, that was my nan. I sucked in a deep breath and forced myself to read the next couple lines.

I know what I did to you was wrong and that you'll probably never forgive me. You don't owe me anything, but I have no one left to turn to.

. . .

That sounded awful. What had the letter writer done? And if it was so bad, why had she kept this letter tucked away all these years? I would definitely be asking Nan, but first I had to get through this short but apparently earth-shattering missive.

Don't punish little Laura for my mistakes.

Laura was my mother's name. Could she be the "little Laura" in question? Oh my gosh. What had happened? What did this mean?

Give her a chance at a better life, at the life we always dreamed of living together.

. . .

Oh my gosh. Oh my gosh. Oh my gosh. I almost stopped right there, but it was too late. The cat was already half out of the bag. I might as well get it all the way out into the open.

I'll be home on leave in two weeks' time and will wait for you in our place that Thursday night.

A secret meeting. Did she go? If so, what happened? What did he want? Was it a he? It seemed that way with the reference to the life they'd dreamed about living together. There was just one little line left, which I read with teary eyes.

Please be the better person. Please come.
W. McAllister

. . .

I finished reading, even more confused than before I'd started. Who was W. McAllister and what had he wanted with my nan? Did he know my mom? Was she the Laura in the letter?

"I found this in there, too." Pringle raised another sheet of paper my way. Apparently he'd collected it while I'd been engrossed in the letter.

Of course, I recognized the official nature of the document right away. It boasted an intricate colored border and at the top of the page read Certificate of Live Birth.

The mother was named as Marilyn Jones, and the father had been listed as William McAllister, most likely the same W. McAllister that had written the letter to Nan. The place of birth was that same unknown town in Georgia, and the baby had been named Laura—my mother's name.

The date of birth matched my mom's, too. It had to be her.

Did this mean that she had never really been Nan's?

That I wasn't Nan's, either?

And what was with this all going down in Georgia? Nan had spoken fondly of her memories growing up in the south, but she'd claimed to be from one of the Carolinas.

Not Georgia. Never Georgia.

And if she'd fibbed about her home state, then what else might she have lied about over the years?

Oh my gosh, did my mom know about any of this? If not, she'd be devastated to learn now. Should I tell her? Or wait until I knew more first?

I had so many questions, and short of tracking down this William McAllister, there was only one person I could ask.

I marched into the house, letter and birth certificate in hand, to confront Nan and demand the truth.

CHAPTER TEN

Nan and Charles sat in the living room, sipping on matching mugs of hot cocoa topped with giant heaps of marshmallow fluff. He wasn't a big fan of tea, so Nan kept this alternate hot drink around mostly just for him.

Paisley had cuddled into Nan's side, and Octo-Cat sat on his favorite perch looking out the window. More than likely, he'd been keeping tabs on me this whole time.

They all looked so cozy and content. I almost felt bad for disturbing that peaceful moment, but then I remembered that I was the one who'd been wronged, lied to. And for my entire life. Wow.

I stood frozen at the edge of the living room, the birth certificate and letter clutched between shaking hands. Where could I possibly begin?

"Hey! You can't just take people's things without asking!" Pringle cried from the foyer. Apparently, he'd followed me inside despite our rule that he wasn't allowed in the house. That snapped me right out of my deer-in-headlights moment.

And I turned on him so fast, he reared back in fright. "Are you really lecturing me on decorum right now?" I demanded, hand on hip. "You can't expect things from others when you're not willing to do the same for them."

Charles set his mug onto the coffee table and approached me carefully. "Angie, is everything all right, sweetie?"

"No, it's not!" I fumed, hating that I'd yelled at him now, too. None of this was his fault. Or Octo-Cat's. Or Paisley's. Or really even Pringle's.

"What's that you have, dear?" Nan asked, remaining seated firmly in her favorite chair. It was her. She'd caused the pain that threatened to rip my heart right in two. The very same woman who'd taught me the importance of honesty as a child had lied to me my entire life.

"I don't know. Why don't you tell me?" I strode over to her and dropped both pieces of paper into her lap.

My grandmother froze. It seemed as if even her heart stopped beating for a moment before she gingerly plucked the papers from her lap and set them on the coffee table. "I haven't the foggiest," she told me as she calmly delivered both mugs to the kitchen sink and then started up the stairs.

"Oh, no!" I shouted, charging after her. "You are not getting away that easily! What is this, and why didn't I know about it? Does mom know about it?"

Nan remained silent as she climbed the steps at her normal pace. It was almost as if I weren't there at all.

"Hey, why aren't you answering me?" I demanded as a new wave of tears began to sting my eyes.

Nan reached her bedroom door, then

turned back to me. Her voice was quiet and almost completely devoid of emotion as she said, "I'm sorry, dear, but I'm not feeling too terribly well all of a sudden. I think I'll just excuse myself to bed for the evening."

Before I could argue, she slipped into the room and clicked the door shut behind her. Still shocked by what I'd learned, and even more so by the fact that my normally talkative grandmother refused to discuss it with me, I twisted the knob hard and pulled.

But it wouldn't budge.

Locked out by my own grandmother!

I pounded on the door instead. "You're going to have to talk about it with me eventually!" I shouted into the wooden barrier.

A warm hand brushed my arm, causing me to jump in my skin.

"C'mon," Charles said, gently guiding me back toward the grand staircase. "It seems like you both could use some space to work things out right about now."

"Did you read it?" I asked through the hot tears that flowed freely now. "Did you read the letter?"

He nodded, his mouth a tight bow.

"What do you think it means?" I asked, my voice cracking partway through that awful question.

"I hate to guess at it." His voice remained soft, comforting. "It'd be much better if we heard from Nan directly."

I let out a bitter laugh. "Well, she doesn't seem to be too keen on sharing. Do you think this means she's not my real nan?"

"Of course, she's your real nan. She raised you. She's been there your whole life. The letter—whatever it means—it doesn't change anything."

"What about my mom, though? Is she the Laura on the birth certificate? Is that what the letter is about? Did her dad give her to Nan for some reason? And does her real mom even know what happened to her?" It was all too horrible to even think about. Unfortunately, I couldn't stop doing just that.

Charles sat on the couch and opened his arms, inviting me to cuddle against him. "I know it's all so confusing and upsetting right now, but I promise you it will be okay. Whatever this is, it doesn't change who your nan is, who you are."

I laughed again. Angry. "If it's no big deal, then why would she keep it a secret all these years? Why would she refuse to talk about it now?"

"I don't know the answers to those questions, but I'll be here to help you figure them out for yourself." He pressed a warm kiss to my forehead.

"I can't," I sobbed, all my hot-headed energy ebbing away.

Charles just hugged me tighter. "What do you mean you can't? You're Angie Russo, Pet Whisperer P.I. You're the woman who solved her first official case in less than an hour. That's pretty incredible."

Oh, yeah, I guess Julie's case was solved. Pringle had admitted to taking the mail and banging up the mailboxes. All I had to do is offer him something he wanted more than whatever secrets he thought he might find, and he'd be sure to stop.

Case solved. Whoop-de-do.

I tried to smile but couldn't. Instead,

Charles held me as I cried into his nicely pressed work shirt.

The one person I'd trusted most in this entire world had kept something monumental from me. If I couldn't rely on her to be honest with me, then who could I count on?

Charles stroked my hair and made soothing noises, reminding me that there was at least one person in my corner, no matter what.

Octo-Cat jumped onto the couch beside me and licked my hand tentatively. Okay, one person and one cat—and probably one dog, too. Though I had no doubt Paisley was busy comforting Nan right about now.

I ran my fingers through Octo-Cat's silky fur, appreciating his friendship more than ever in that moment.

"Angela, I can see you are quite upset," he murmured, proving just how far we'd come since fate first flung us together. "Does this mean we're out of Evian?"

Leave it to my cat to put things into stark perspective.

"No. Don't worry," I said with a chuckle,

feeling lighter already. "We have plenty of Evian."

I scratched him between the ears and then pulled myself up from the couch. A nice cool glass of Evian would do us all good right about then.

CHAPTER ELEVEN

Despite the night cap of perfectly chilled Evian, I had a hard time drifting to sleep. Sometime early the next morning, I gave up on getting any meaningful shut-eye and went to see if Nan was up yet.

Oh, not only was she up…

She was already gone—and with her little dog, too. Darn, I could have used Paisley's eternal sense of optimism to help get me through what I knew was going to be a tough day.

Well, it's not like Nan and Paisley would be gone forever. Eventually, they had to come back. Eventually, the woman who was maybe not my actual grandmother would have to give me some answers. After all, Pringle had given me undeniable evidence that something wasn't quite right about our family past, and even though I was one whole generation removed from whatever scandal Nan had worked so hard to keep hidden, it still upset me deeply.

Octo-Cat sat waiting for me on the kitchen counter. Nan didn't like it when he dirtied her food prep surfaces, but I hadn't the heart or the inclination to correct him—especially not today.

"Good morning, Angela," he said, making eyes toward his empty food bowl. "You're right on time for my morning repast."

"C'mon," I mumbled as I shuffled toward the pantry and extracted a can of Fancy Feast. I also grabbed a clean Lenox teacup and matching saucer, the only dishes he was willing to eat or drink from. After setting both on the floor, I grabbed the half-empty bottle of Evian from the fridge and poured it into the delicate filigreed teacup until it was exactly three-fourths full.

During our time together, he'd learned to appreciate the nuanced flavor of chilled water, and I'd learned not to question his sometimes ridiculous standards and completely non-optional routines.

"Many thanks," he mumbled before digging in with aplomb.

I grabbed a Diet Coke from the fridge since Nan wasn't around to make coffee, and I didn't feel like dealing with my deep-rooted fear of getting electrocuted on top of everything else so early in the day.

"So what's on our schh-edule for today?" my cat asked, over-emphasizing his speech as he often liked to do when he was feeling fancy—usually in the mornings and usually post-Fancy Feast.

I considered his question for a few moments. Of course, I already knew exactly what we needed to do, but that didn't mean I liked it. He probably wouldn't, either, but there was no time like the present.

I forced a smile. "We need to talk to

Pringle and see what it will take to get him to help us."

Octo-Cat groaned, refusing to even pretend he liked this plan. "Do we have to?"

"It's the quickest, most surefire way to figure out what Nan's hiding, especially since she doesn't seem to want to talk about it."

"I did find it a little strange how quickly she ran out of here this morning." His voice became deep, cold, as he cast his eyes toward the floor. "She didn't even stop to give me a pet hello."

Poor guy. There was nothing he hated more than being ignored when he wanted attention. Of course, that had never stopped him from ignoring me when it suited him to do so. Double standards were just a part of being a cat owner, and I'd accepted that a long time ago.

"Nan's always been a lot strange, but she's also always been honest and upfront. At least that's what I thought." I sighed and took another sip from my can of Diet Coke. Yes, I knew he was hurting from that morning's slight, but I was hurting, too—and if you asked me, it was for far bigger, far more painful reasons.

My cat studied me with large amber eyes. "You're really upset by this, aren't you?"

I nodded and sighed again. "I really am."

He moaned as if in terrible agony. "Well, that won't do. Let's go rouse the raccoon and get this over with." He traipsed out of the kitchen, his tail held high as he led the way to his electronic pet door and slipped outside.

Aww, he really did love me. Sometimes I still wondered about that, given his hot and cold behavior when it came to pretty much everything he ever encountered. But today his willingness to do something that mildly annoyed him in order to mend my badly broken heart gave me all kinds of warm fuzzies.

When I joined him outside on the porch, he sat and motioned with one paw toward the giant gaping hole that led into Pringle's lair. "Well, go ahead."

I approached slowly, my voice soft, beseeching. "Pringle?"

"What do you want?" the raccoon growled from somewhere under his porch. Actually, it was my porch. Must not forget that.

"I was wondering if you could help us get to the bottom of that secret you shared with me last night?" I begged.

If my cat's moods ran hot and cold, Pringle wavered between the freezing and boiling points on that same wretched thermometer. His warm was almost angry, though. In fact, did we really need his help? Was it worth dealing with his attitude and trickery?

Yes, I realized, my heart dropping to the ground. Yes, we did need him. Darn it.

He poked his head out of the hole and grimaced. "Actually, I'm not very happy with you right now." That was unexpected.

"What? Why?" I was already having a hard time coming to him hat in hands. If I had to spend half the morning groveling and begging, we'd never make any progress at all.

He rubbed his temples and squinted hard against the rising sun. Well, at least we both gave each other headaches.

"I wasn't giving you the papers," he explained with a tired yet demanding voice. "I showed them to you to see, not to keep. I refuse to help until you give back what's mine."

Octo-Cat came galloping over with impressive speed. "Excuse you? Don't those papers actually belong to Nan? Didn't you steal them away from her in the first place?"

"Not helping," I groaned, nudging Octo-Cat gently to the side with my foot, a slight I knew I'd pay for later. "I'm sorry, Pringle. That was really rude of me. I was just in such shock that I forgot. I'll go get them for you right now."

When I returned with the letter and birth certificate in hand, Pringle was waiting on the porch.

"I'll take those," he said, yanking them away even though I would've given them to him freely. He tucked both into his armpit and crossed his arms over his chest. "Now, how can I help you? Make it snappy. I'm a very busy animal, you know."

I nodded toward the papers he'd stashed within his gray fur. "Those told part of a secret, but not the whole thing. I need to know the rest. Can you help?"

He cocked his head to the side and sighed heavily. "That depends."

Octo-Cat hissed and raised the hair on his back. "Depends? Depends! Stop being a furry jerk wad and help already. You started this!"

"Madame, please control your associate." He shook his head as if this all pained him greatly.

"Octo-Cat, I've got this," I told him with an apologetic smile, then turned back to the raccoon with what I was sure had to be a very poorly concealed grimace. "Go ahead, Pringle."

The raccoon walked a few paces, then turned his face over his shoulder dramatically and sized me up. "I'm not sure how much you get around the forest these days, but I'm not just some amateur gumshoe. I'm a legitimate business animal now."

Octo-Cat exploded upon hearing this claim. "I don't believe this. Does he reall—"

As much as I hated to do it, I pushed my best feline friend through the pet door and then blocked it with my leg. "You're in business?" I asked peaceably.

He nodded animatedly; his chest puffed with pride. "Yes, indeed. You're looking at the proud owner and key talent behind Pringle Whisperer, P.I. I'll have you know that it's the very best investigation firm in the area."

I pinched the skin on the inside of my wrist to stop myself from saying something snarky. I had no idea this masked thief stole ideas and business models in addition to papers and trinkets. I also hugely resented the implication that his P.I. outfit was superior to the one I ran with Octo-Cat. But, ugh, I still needed his help.

"Congratulations," I managed, thinking it was a good thing I had pushed Octo-Cat in through the cat door, otherwise there would be a definite brawl right about now. "So can I hire you to help me out here?"

He smiled wide, revealing two rows of

gleaming, pointed teeth. "Of course you can, princess. But it'll come at a price."

"You're going to charge me?" I balked, remembering the stack of pretty green bills he planned to use for origami. He didn't even know what cash was, let alone its value, considering he had a tendency to just take anything he wanted. "What do you even need money for?"

He rubbed his thumb and index finger together. "Not money. Favors."

I took a moment to soak this in. When I'd promised Octo-Cat a favor in exchange for his cooperation, I'd ended up with the giant manor house that had once belonged to his late owner. I'd grown to love our new house, but it was still a steep price to pay for getting him to agree to wear a cheap pet harness one time.

"Well," Pringle prompted me, reminding me that I still hadn't responded to his heinous offer. "Are you in or out?"

Oh, I knew I would come to regret this, but I also knew I needed him and that the longer I went without untangling Nan's secrets, the more desperate I would become.

"Fine." I squatted down and offered him my index finger, which he promptly accepted and shook in agreement.

"Excellent. Then it seems we've got ourselves a deal," Pringle said, steepling his fingers in true villain fashion.

Well, at least he was on my side this time. Um, right?

CHAPTER TWELVE

My deal with the sometimes downright devilish raccoon made, I opened the front door wide and invited him to join us inside.

"I've never been so insulted in all my life," Octo-Cat grumbled, apparently having overheard our entire conversation from the other side of the blocked pet door. "And don't you know better than to make an open-ended bargain with a crook?"

Pringle bared his teeth. "You know, I used to like you," he spat at the cat. "Idolize you, even. Pffft. Pathetic."

"Oh, and now you don't? I'm so hurt," my cat snarked right back. These two were pretty well-matched when it came to conversational gymnastics. It was a shame the only thing they wanted to do was fight each other rather than work together.

I had to do something to get everyone back on track. Perhaps asking nicely would do the trick?

"Guys, that's enough," I said with a stern look. "Like it or not, we need to work together on this one. I need you to put your differences aside and recognize that we're all the same team here."

"At least one of you has a bit of sense," Pringle said, shooting a dirty look toward Octo-Cat. Sigh.

Much to my surprise and delight, the tabby stayed quiet. His wildly flicking tail belied his true feelings, though.

I offered him an appreciative smile before moving forward with the plan. "Let's get started in the attic. Pringle, can you show me the hiding place you mentioned the other night? The one in the baseboards?"

He nodded and gave me the thumbs up sign. I swear he was becoming more human by the day. "Sure. I'll meet you up there," he said.

"Um, can't we just go up together?" I stood and pointed toward the stairs. "I mean, it's just up there."

He raised both eyebrows and shot me a goofy grin. "We could, but I prefer to use my private entrance. Remember, I'm VIP, honey. Very Important Pringle."

"Gag me on my own hairball," Octo-Cat grumbled. I wouldn't just owe Pringle after this. I was starting to think my cat would deserve a medal for his restraint in dealing with the obnoxious forest animal.

"Fine," I said even though I was already beyond irritated. I opened the front door for the raccoon so that he could sashay his way outside, then grabbed a folding chair from the storage closet and marched upstairs to the guest room where I'd found Nan Marie Kondo-ing the other day.

"Let me help you," I told the tabby in light of the nasty spill he'd taken last time we were up here.

"Don't insult me." He jumped onto the

chair, wiggled his butt, and leaped through the hatch flawlessly.

I followed shortly after, also using the chair to help me gain an adequate amount of leverage before pulling myself up by my throbbing arms.

Once I was seated securely on the attic floor, I glanced around the space, surprised by the high ceilings—although I probably shouldn't have been given the general grandeur of the estate. Even in the rarely visited space, the floors were made of elegant hardwood, and the walls had been decorated in a pretty green, textured wallpaper. One hexagonal window sat within the far wall, casting a steady beam of light into the space.

Pringle was already there waiting for us. "Took you long enough."

"Show us the hiding place," I commanded, no longer worried about being courteous with the sarcastic, self-important under-porch dweller. We just needed to get on with business.

He nodded and walked around the edge of the room before stopping in the corner farthest from the window. "Here," he said, pointing.

I dropped to my knees and pulled at the edge of the wood trim, but it remained firmly wedged in place.

"It's push, champ. Not pull," Pringle explained, giving it a swift karate kick. Sure enough, the mahogany trim collapsed to reveal a dark hole.

I gulped down my nerves and reached my hand into the mysterious space.

Nothing.

"I already cleaned it out," the raccoon revealed. "Nothing left. Not in there at least."

"Then what are we even doing up here?" Octo-Cat demanded with a huff. It was only then I realized he was pacing the length of the room.

"Look." Pringle pointed toward a stack of cardboard boxes nearby. "There are some new things here since I last searched."

"Nan's Marie Kondo-ing," I whispered. "She wasn't just throwing things out. She was hiding them here, too."

Pringle rubbed his hands together in

excitement. "Oooh, fun. Let's go see what new secrets we can find."

I opened each of the three boxes and set them side by side on the floor. Pringle immediately dove into the biggest one while I decided to start with the smallest.

"It's times like this I think it might be nice to have fingers, even though they look so… yuck." Octo-Cat shuddered at the thought, then stalked over to lie in the sunbeam coming from the window, leaving us to do all the snooping.

The first box I tried held a delicate collection of Christmas ornaments, all lovingly kept. Not one thing even remotely suspicious.

I moved to the next box and found Nan's favorite summer looks tucked away for safe keeping now that it was getting cold. Also nothing that helped with our search into the hidden past.

"What have you found?" I asked Pringle when I realized he still hadn't emerged from the giant box.

"Huh? What?" He popped his head over the cardboard flap with a sheepish grin. One of Nan's silk patterned scarves had been tied over his ears, and several pieces of costume jewelry lay against his furry chest. "Oh, nothing about the case. Just a small part of my P.I. fee."

Octo-Cat sighed heavily but remained blessedly quiet.

"No, no more stealing," I hissed, feeling a bit like an animal myself. The more human they became, the less like a person I felt myself. "Put it all back."

"You're no fun. You know that?" The dejected raccoon at least followed orders without arguing my instructions any further. He made sad, disparaging noises as he removed each piece of glittering finery.

"Okay, well. That didn't exactly help anything," I said once I was sure every last item had been returned to the boxes from which they came.

We each exited through the floor hatch and stood together in the guest room discussing next steps.

"What about Nan's room?" Octo-Cat suggested. "Should we search there?"

Pringle clapped and did a happy little jump. "Oh, yes, yes, yes. Let's do that!"

Normally, I'd hate to invade my nan's privacy, but desperate times and all that… and I was very, very desperate to finally learn the truth that had eluded me since long before I'd even been born. "Let's give it a try," I acquiesced.

We marched in a single-file line down the hall toward Nan's bedroom, but when I reached the door, it was still locked up tight.

"Want me to break in?" Pringle offered, making grippy-grabby gestures with his hands. I wondered, not for the first time, whether I'd be able to find a vet to prescribe my raccoon neighbor a daily dose of Ritalin for his obvious ADHD. Mmm, probably not.

"I shouldn't have any problem jimmying the lock on the window," he continued, bouncing on all four legs now.

"No," I said, feeling both guilty and disappointed in equal measures. "Nan will be back eventually. Let me try to talk to her first. Maybe she's had enough time to cool down. Maybe tonight she'll be ready to talk."

"Hey, now wait just a minute here!" Pringle cried in distress. "Even if that happens, you still owe me my payment. Remember, I'm a legitimate business animal now, and we made an unbreakable deal when you hired me earlier today."

"That's it. I've had enough," Octo-Cat said, heading upstairs toward our tower bedroom, and I had to agree with him there. So much time in the raccoon's company had me feeling like I'd just run three marathons back-to-back… but with my patience instead of my muscles.

"I'll come get you when we're ready for the next steps," I told him as I guided him back outside. As soon as he exited the house, I shut the door tight and took a deep breath.

Oh, Nan. Please put me out of my misery. All you need to do is talk to me, and we can put an end to all of this.

CHAPTER THIRTEEN

Despite many fervent prayers sent Heavenward, Nan didn't talk to me that night. In fact, she didn't even come back home. How do I know? Because I set up camp in the living room and waited all night, that's how.

Of course, now I only had more questions than before.

Was she out doing damage control or simply hiding from me to avoid a confrontation? And where had she even gone?

Desperate for answers, I called my mom the next morning.

"Angie, good morning! It's so good to hear from you!" my mom chirped in such a delighted tone that I instantly knew Nan hadn't turned up at her place.

I had a choice to make then. I could tell her everything and invite her to help, or I could stay silent.

Even though our relationship had become closer ever since I let her in on my secret ability to communicate with animals, I worried about what this new revelation would do to our relationship. Either she'd known all this time and had also chosen to keep the truth of our lineage hidden from me, or she had no idea and would be shattered by the news.

Frankly, I didn't like either option.

"Hi, Mom," I said, my mind made up. "Just calling to say hi on my way to the electronics store. Need anything while I'm out?"

"Oh, that's so nice of you to offer, but your father and I are fine." She sounded so happy. I really need to call her more, to invite her over here or swing by her place.

I smiled, hoping she'd be able to hear it in my voice. "Okay, just wanted to be sure. Love you, Mom."

"I love you, too, baby."

We hung up and I squeezed the phone in my hand, drawing strength from its warmth. I needed to learn whatever truth Nan was hiding. I owed it to not just myself, but my mom, too.

"What happens next?" Octo-Cat wanted to know then.

"Stay here and keep an eye out for Nan," I told him, even more determined than before to get to the bottom of this—and fast. "I need to pick up some equipment."

"Does this mean…?" His eyes grew large as his words trailed away.

"We're breaking into that room," I confirmed. "At least you and Pringle are."

"Well, you know what they say. Keep your friends close and your enemies closer." He crossed his paws daintily, then nodded toward the remote. "Turn the tube on for me, will you?"

I grabbed the remote as requested, but didn't turn on the TV just yet.

"Let's get on with it, please, Angela," my cat groaned.

"One thing first." I took a deep breath to

steady myself, knowing he wouldn't like what I said next. "I need you to understand that I will not be buying Apple products for our mission today."

He jumped up onto all four feet, his fur puffed in distress. "What? Why?"

Yes, my cat was a major brand loyalist—Apple, Evian, Fancy Feast, Lenox—the guy had standards and stuck to them.

"Sometimes they don't have what we need," I explained gently. "But don't worry. Pringle's the one who will be using the new stuff. You don't have to."

He sighed and settled back into a comfortable position. "Then it's all for the best. That raccoon doesn't deserve i-Anything."

This made me laugh. Crisis averted. "Right!"

"Now would you, please, turn on the television?" he asked with an irritated flick of his tail.

"Sure, yeah." I clicked the TV on to the movie channel and their current broadcast of When Harry Met Sally, then blew him a quick kiss before heading toward the door. "I'll be back."

"Hasta la vista, baby." He dropped his voice so it became deep, but nowhere deep enough to deliver that famous quote properly. Luckily, I was able to keep my giggles inside until I'd slammed the car door behind me and began the trek to the big box electronics store.

Last time I'd stopped by had been to buy a GPS pet tracker for our squirrel friend Maple. I'd come one time before as well; it had been to buy an Apple Watch for Octo-Cat, although for the life of me I couldn't remember why I needed one or what ever happened to it. I knew Maple's GPS had ended up buried somewhere in the forest like one of the manic squirrel's nuts or half-eaten jars of peanut butter. And, yes, I was her supplier against my better judgement.

"Hey, I know you!" A pimply faced employee with curly hair and a brightly colored polo shirt approached while laughing. He was the same one who'd helped me the first time I came in looking to equip the animals with their own spy tech.

"How did your cat like his Apple Watch?" He made air quotes around Apple since we'd actually bought an off-brand product and stuck the preferred logo over top. Shoot. Sometimes I was way too free with information about my crazy life.

"It was great. Thanks." I'd been lucky enough not to run into him on my second visit, which meant I'd gotten in and out of there in mere minutes. It seemed today I wouldn't be quite so lucky.

"Are you here for a new MacBook Pro or an iPad Air? Maybe a matching Apple Watch for your dog?"

"No, she doesn't need a watch," I muttered, and the store clerk laughed even harder. I wasn't a violent person by nature, but I also kind of wanted to punch him in the face. Did he really think it was a good idea to tease and bully his customers? Perhaps corporate would like to hear about my experience today. Hmm.

He sobered at last, placing both hands in his pockets and turning to me with an open expression. Maybe now that he'd gotten his laughs in, he'd actually help here. "Okay. What can I get for you?"

I offered a pert smile. "I need a GoPro camera, please, and a harness to go with it."

Again, raucous laughter. "Oh, so your cat likes Apple, but your dog likes GoPro?" He could barely get the words out because he was wheezing so hard.

"Actually, it's for my raccoon, but yeah." I smiled wide just to unnerve him. He already thought I was crazy, so I might as well lean into it.

Sure enough, the next thing out of his mouth was, "You're weird, you know that?"

"And you're not very helpful, so I guess I'll just help myself. Thank you!" I called over my shoulder, already walking away.

"Hang on. GoPros are this way." He darted past me and hooked a right. "You need a key to get into the case, which means you do need my help."

"Fine, but I'm in a hurry."

"Urgent animal business?" he guessed, holding back another laugh.

"Something like that," I answered. Fine, whatever. He could make fun of me all he wanted. As long as I got the camera and harness, I'd go about my day just fine.

"Good luck!" he called after me once he'd handed over the equipment I requested. Yeah, like I needed his well wishes—or like he even meant them in the first place. Next time I'd be finding a different electronics store, even if I had to drive twice as far to get to it.

I gave the bully clerk a thumbs up as I approached the cash register, refusing to look back or say another word. I had far bigger problems to worry about today.

Nan was missing.

My mom probably had different parents than she'd been led to believe.

I owed a raccoon of questionable ethics an unspoken favor.

Oh, and also, I was about to spy on my own grandmother in a desperate attempt to learn the truth behind it all...

CHAPTER FOURTEEN

Apparently, my trip to the electronics store had gone by much more quickly than it felt. When I arrived home, Octo-Cat sat watching the final scene of his movie and sniffling mightily.

"Aww, does somebody love love?" I teased. He never reacted this way to Law & Order.

"Of course, not!" he cried, wiping at his eyes to hide the telltale signs of tears. "I'm laughing. Yeah. Still laughing. I'll have what she's having. Classic!"

"Uh-huh," I said, keeping my smile on the inside. Although I knew for a fact he had no idea what that famous scene actually referenced, I decided to let him off the hook this time. The last thing I needed was to have the birds and bees talk with my neutered cat. Nope, no thank you!

Instead, I focused on unpackaging and setting up the new GoPro while Harry danced with Sally at the New Year's Eve party and told her all the things he loved best about her. So super sweet. Okay, maybe now I was tearing up a little, too.

When the end credits finally rolled, I switched off the television and opened the front door. "C'mon, Pringle. It's time!"

The raccoon came trotting right in, ready to go, as if he'd been standing outside the door waiting this entire time. Perhaps, he had.

Spotting the new tech in my hands, he gasped and lifted both hands to his mouth, then dropped them and shouted, "Oooh, shiny!"

He then wrapped both hands around my calf and shimmied right up my body and onto my shoulder. He'd never done that before, and I didn't want him to be doing it now. Even though we were working together, I still didn't exactly trust him.

Luckily, I overcame my shock just in time to stop him from stealing the camera out of my hands and making a fast getaway with the clearly coveted device.

"Stop that," I groused and shook my arms. "Get off of me."

"I want that," Pringle informed me, refusing to be shaken off.

"Relax, will you? I bought it for you to use in today's mission."

"Give! Give! Give!" He climbed back to the floor, then jumped up and down, becoming increasingly annoying by the second.

"You need to give it a rest," Octo-Cat intervened. "Let Angela do her little speech first, then she'll give it to you."

"Oh, so now I'm predictable?" I asked with a chuckle. I'm not exactly sure why I laughed in that moment, but it probably had to do with how relieved I was to have the giant raccoon back on the floor and off my body.

"It's not just you, honey," Pringle said.

"It's all humans. Such simple creatures." He made a rolling gesture with his hands and sighed. "Anyway, just get on with it."

Oh, this was rich. Mr. Must Maintain His Schedule to the Very Second and Mr. Steal Everything in Sight found me to be the predictable one.

Also, was Pringle really mocking me when I'd hired him and also agreed to pay an unnamed favor? That wasn't very good customer service. He was lucky his business wasn't on Yelp, or he'd be getting a very bad review.

"Haven't you ever heard that the customer's always right?" I asked with a snort.

"Nope. Who would say that?" Pringle chittered with unabashed glee. "The customer's often stupid, which is why they need to hire help to begin with."

Yikes. Yet another astute comment on humanity from the Peeping Tom raccoon. Thank goodness he couldn't communicate with any humans other than me.

But really, we needed to get on with our mission here, which meant it was time for me to lay down the law. "Hush up and listen already!" I yelled at them both.

When they both fell silent, I continued. "Now, Octo-Cat, you're going to like this next part."

I lifted my phone from the table and unlocked it to show the new app I'd downloaded during setup. "Pringle's going to wear the camera in a chest harness, and I'm going to stream the live feed to my iPhone so I can keep an eye on what's happening."

"Okay, but where do I fit into this plan?" my cat asked with an aggravated twitch.

"Two places." I made a peace sign and wiggled those two fingers, unsure whether either animal could count, but whatever. "First, you're going to go with Pringle to keep an eye on him and make sure he doesn't take anything that's unrelated to our case."

"Hey," the raccoon whined. "I resemble that remark."

I rolled my eyes and took a deep breath. Sometimes I really missed working at the law firm with other humans—sweet, rational humans. "Second, we're going to use your iPad to FaceTime so you can give me a running commentary to go with the video feed. I'd give you my phone, but I think the buttons would be too tiny to answer with your paws, and I don't want to take any chances, so—"

"Wait, wait, wait," Octo-Cat slurred, his eyes growing large and greedy. "Are you going to use your iPad or your iPhone to keep tabs on us?"

"Both," I said with a smile.

"It's like Christmas and my birthday and Halloween all rolled into one," he gushed in that accented tone of his.

I nodded vigorously and reached out to pat him on the head. "Yup. Fun, right? We're all having fun? Yes? Now, Pringle, if you're ready, I can outfit you in the harness now."

The raccoon grabbed the camera and turned it over several times in his hands, then gave me an exaggerated wink. "This is some next-level spy stuff. I didn't know you had it in you."

"Yeah, well, I'm just full of surprises. And as it turns out, so is Nan. Do you both understand the mission?" I asked as I held the harness up to Pringle's upper body to get a read on how tight I'd need to make the straps.

The cat and raccoon nodded in unison.

"Octo-Cat, where's your iPad?" I asked as I finished fastening the harness around Pringle's chest, then mounted the camera on his back and tested the feed on my phone.

"Dining room table," the tabby answered and then went with me to retrieve it. "Say, why aren't you going in there with us?"

"It just feels like too big an invasion of privacy," I admitted.

"But you're still going to see everything through the feed, so how is that different?" Octo-Cat deadpanned.

I shrugged. "I don't know. It just is."

Thankfully, he dropped it without playing twenty questions as to my motive. "Fair enough."

"Thanks for understanding." I opened the door that led outside again.

"Okay, Pringle, do your thing. Get on the roof, unlock the window, and then come back down to grab the iPad. I'll leave it right here for you," I said, setting it on the edge of the porch.

"Octo-Cat, come with me." He followed me upstairs to our library office, and I opened the large bay window so he could slink onto the roof.

"I'll wait five minutes to give you two time to get into the room, then I'll call you on FaceTime," I called after him. "Make sure you answer."

"Roger that," my cat said, turning to glance at me over his shoulder and offering an agreeable smile before disappearing from sight.

This was it. Either we'd soon find some of the answers I'd been searching for… or we'd be nearly out of places we could look.

Unfortunately, if the animals didn't turn up anything in their search, I had no idea what we'd do next. It was looking more and more like I'd need to choose to let it go or force a confrontation with Nan.

Yay, me.

CHAPTER FIFTEEN

I headed outside to the front porch, both because I knew it would offer me better reception and so that I could keep an eye out for Nan just in case she finally decided to return home and face the situation head-on.

After settling myself on the steps, I took out my phone and studied the feed from our Pringle cam. I could see his focused expression reflected back in the glass as he fiddled with the window. His eyes lit up a few moments later as he raised the window high enough for Octo-Cat to squeeze through, then turned back the other way, providing me with an impressive aerial view of the forest that flanked our yard.

Fast as a shot, he appeared at my side and grabbed Octo-Cat's iPad from the stoop. "I'll be taking that now. Thank you very much."

For all his issues, the raccoon really was a great accomplice with an impressive skill set. It was also far easier on my conscience to let him do the dirty work so that I wouldn't have to.

Pringle, of course, had no trouble bending the rules of propriety or in scaling the house with the tablet tucked into his chest and held in place by one furry black hand. Hardly a minute later, he'd made it back to Nan's window, raised it a bit higher, and entered the locked bedroom without even a second's hesitation.

This was it. We were really doing it. I grabbed my iPad and placed a FaceTime call to Octo-Cat.

He answered after a few rings, his face leaning over the device and showing me the same view of kitty double chin I got any morning I dared try to sleep in past his breakfast time. "Badges. We don't need no stinking badges," he informed me needlessly.

And what was with all these movie quotes? Did he even sleep anymore or just fill his brain with anything that would fit inside?

"Good job," I told him, finding his enthusiasm adorable despite everything. "Keep an eye on Pringle, and keep me informed as you two search the room."

"Yes, Angela. I remember my role in all this," he murmured, already moving out of view.

Pringle had already made his way to Nan's dresser and was pulling open drawers willy-nilly. "Lacy underwear!" he cried with a giggle. "Oh, Nan, I had no idea!"

"Cut that out!" I shouted so loud they could probably hear me without the FaceTime connection. "You're there to look for clues, and that's it."

"Open this for me," I heard Octo-Cat say and then watched as Pringle approached the spot where my cat waited by the nightstand.

The raccoon pulled the drawer clear off the tracks and laughed as it clattered to the floor. "This is fun!" he squealed.

Well, there would be no hiding the fact we'd been in her room, even though I technically hadn't.

"Hey, look! I found a piece of paper with writing on it!" my cat cried in excitement.

Pringle bounded over and grabbed the paper, but I couldn't make out the words on the camera as the raccoon read. "It's just an old shopping list," he said, balling it up and tossing it back in the drawer. I sure hoped his assessment was right and he hadn't just discarded an important piece of the puzzle.

Maybe I should just go up there and instruct the two of them on how they could unlock the door from inside. Still, I remained frozen in place, unable to cross that invisible boundary.

"Be respectful of my nan's things!" I cried in a half-hearted attempt to exert some control over the situation.

"Why?" Pringle asked in a distracted voice as he continued to lope around the bedroom. "Think about it. Was she respectful of you when she hid such an important truth just out of reach?"

Darn him and his logical points.

"Still," I muttered. "Just, please."

"You heard the lady!" Octo-Cat growled. "Keep it professional here."

Oh, how I loved my kitty. He was definitely the next best thing to being there myself, and I was proud of him for staying on task.

The fuzzy duo searched around the room a while longer, finding nothing of consequence.

"If she's hiding anything, it wouldn't be in an obvious place," I said, trying to help from my station outside the action. "The attic hiding place was pretty cleverly tucked away. Maybe there's a similar hiding place in her room, too."

"Good thinking," Pringle said and then lumbered over to the nearest baseboard. He kicked and punched to no avail; not a single board budged.

"Hey! I think I found something!" Octo-Cat shouted from across the room. Oh my gosh. Was this it? The moment of truth?

"Coming!" Pringle called. The camera bounced unevenly as he raced toward Octo-

Cat, who sat on top of the dresser—the first place they'd searched.

At that very same moment, the hum of an engine alerted me to the little red sports car pulling up our driveway.

Nan had come home.

"Mommy, I'm back!" Paisley cried from the open window, and while I was happy to see her, this meant that I had zero time to send a warning message to the guys upstairs.

"Paisley! Nan! Welcome home!" I shouted while closing the video feed and ending the FaceTime call. I hoped the animals engaged in the spy operation upstairs had heard and understood that they needed to get the heck out of there. Subtlety wasn't exactly a strong suit for either of them.

Nan pulled into the garage, and I raced after her before she could run away from me again. Maybe she was finally ready to give me some answers. At the very least, I might be able to distract her long enough to buy some time for Octo-Cat and Pringle to escape.

"I missed you!" Paisley bounded out of

the car and ran over to me, begging to be picked up.

I was all too happy to oblige. "I missed you, too. Both of you."

Nan looked as if she hadn't slept the whole time she'd been gone. Perhaps she hadn't. Still, she attempted a reserved smile. Of course, the Nan I knew had never been reserved a day in her life. What had happened to her, and why was it all coming to a head now?

"Are you okay?" I asked gently.

She shook her head. "Not really. No."

"Can we talk about it?" I reached out to put a hand on her shoulder, but she shook me off.

Nan took a deep breath, then retreated into herself. I'd never seen her look so old or broken, and it worried me greatly. Tears rimmed her red eyes. "I never thought I'd have to speak of it again, especially not to you."

"I'm here, and I love you, no matter what."

She shook her head sadly. "It will change things, Angie."

"It already has," I whispered as I attempted to hold back fresh tears of my own.

Nan looked away and murmured, "I can't." Then brushed past me into the house.

Guilt surged inside my chest. Maybe this was one mystery that didn't need to be solved. Maybe I just needed to leave it alone and move on with my life the way things had been before Pringle showed me that secret letter.

I wished I could turn away, but I was already in too deep. This wasn't a simple curiosity; it was my life.

And I needed to know the truth.

CHAPTER SIXTEEN

After Nan abandoned me in the garage, I went back to sit on the porch. Lately, I'd been spending more time out here than inside the house, it seemed.

Paisley ambled after me, wagging her tail as usual, but slowly, cautiously. "What's wrong, Mommy?"

Although she couldn't communicate with Nan like she did me, I still felt uncomfortable saying anything bad about her best friend, the woman who had rescued her from the overcrowded shelter and given her a home.

Where was Nan now? Had she made it to her room? Had she spotted the mess made by the animals and known I was the one to put them up to it? Would she ever forgive me? Could I ever forgive her?

"I just feel sad," I told the sympathetic Chihuahua at last.

"Sometimes I get sad," the little dog said, snuggling onto my lap. "But then you know what I do? I decide to stop being sad and just be happy instead."

I smiled and scratched her between the ears. "That's very smart, Paisley. Hey, did you and Nan have a nice adventure?"

I was more looking for a change of topic than any additional dirt on Nan, but then it occurred to me that if I asked the right questions, Paisley might be able to crack this case wide open. She was with Nan practically every waking hour—slept in her room, too. How much did she pay attention? How much did she know?

She closed her eyes and rolled over on my lap to expose her belly for scratches. "The car ride was great, and I liked smelling the new smells, but I would have rather been home, all of us together."

"Aww, I know how you feel. Where did the two of you go?" I asked, unable to resist.

She squinted one eye open. "I'm not sure. It was a small clean room with a big bed. Nan and I cuddled and slept a lot. We also watched TV quite a bit. I know Octavius likes it, but I think it's pretty boring just watching things happen in a small glass box. I'd much rather be doing them myself."

"Yet another smart observation," I said with a sad smile. It sounded like Nan had holed up in some kind of a motel rather than talk to me. Fabulous.

I sighed and continued to stroke the happy little dog. She trusted so easily, so completely. Why couldn't I be like that? I had no doubt she was the most contented among us, and it wasn't because ignorance was bliss. Paisley was incredibly smart, yet somehow still able to push all her problems to the side and choose happiness each and every day.

We sat like that for a while until Pringle appeared from the side yard and bolted up the steps, which immediately sent Paisley barking.

She bounded off my lap and stood guard

beside me, shouting, "Mommy! Mommy! The big bad raccoon is back!"

The raccoon groaned and shook his head. "Are we really going to do this every time? Every single time?" he asked me with an exhausted huff.

"It's okay, Paisley." I picked her back up and set her on my lap.

She whined but stayed in place.

Pringle came closer, something small and rectangular clutched in one hand.

"What did you find, Pringle?"

The pet door beeped, and Octo-Cat stepped out to join us. "What a thrill!" he exclaimed. "I really thought we were going to be caught there for a second."

Pringle put an arm around the tabby and smiled. "Stick with me, kid. Every day's an adventure."

Both laughed.

Crud. For the sake of this case, it was nice that they'd managed to put their differences aside, but going forward? Pringle wasn't exactly the best influence on my somewhat sweet, somewhat bitter tabby cat.

"Can I see what you have there?" I asked again, reaching out my hand.

"Certainly." The raccoon placed an old photograph in my hand. I immediately recognized a much younger Nan but didn't know the man who stood at her side with a cheesy grin and two deep dimples to match.

"We found it tucked into the corner of the mirror. Right out in the open," Octo-Cat informed me, a self-satisfied smile stretching between his whiskers.

"Go ahead. Flip it over," Pringle urged.

"Dorothy and William, summer 1968," I read aloud and gasped. "William? That's him?"

Pringle nodded and shrugged. "Seems so."

Right out in the open, just as Octo-Cat had said. I probably could have discovered this picture a dozen times if I'd ever stopped to study the collage of keepsakes she kept tucked into the edges of the mirror that hung above her dresser.

"They're holding hands," Octo-Cat pointed out. "Like you and UpChuck do all the time."

"She seems smitten," I said breathlessly as I noticed the way her eyes shone, the coy smile that played at her lips as she stared at him dreamily. "Like she loved him."

"Sad to say, doesn't look like he feels the same way," Pringle pointed out, and he was right about that, too. William stood stiff, his eyes focused in the distance rather than at my lovesick nan.

Octo-Cat traipsed over and sat down beside me. "He's right. When you're with UpChuck, you look just like that." He touched his nose down onto the portrait of Nan. "But so does he. This guy looks happy, but not in love. Not like you and UpChuck or Baby and Johnny. Not even like Harry and Sally, and we all know what a mess their relationship was in the beginning."

"Who are Harry and Sally?" Paisley asked, giving her friend a lick hello.

Octo-Cat rolled his eyes lovingly. "Yeesh. I have a lot to catch you up on, dog," he said as if the events of his movie marathoning were an actual part of real life. Crazy cat.

I glanced back down at the photo and frowned.

Was Nan hiding a broken heart? A sad tale of unrequited love? It still didn't explain the letter or the birth certificate. Had William used his hold on her emotions to make her do something awful?

"Poor Nan," I whispered.

Paisley whined, even though I wasn't sure she knew why we were sad in that moment.

The other two said nothing.

We sat like that for a while as I considered my next move. The animals had been a huge help so far, but I needed a second opinion—a human opinion.

"I'm calling Charles," I informed them. Yes, Charles. He wasn't just the love of my life; he was also the smartest and most hardworking person I knew. He didn't become the youngest law firm partner in Blueberry Bay history by phoning it in.

I was afraid I'd reached a dead end, but maybe he'd be able to shed some new light on these old secrets from the past.

At the very least, he could give me the hug I so desperately needed to give me the strength to keep going.

CHAPTER SEVENTEEN

Charles came home from work early so we could spend the rest of the afternoon and evening going over everything I'd learned during the past couple of days.

"I've been so worried about you," he said now that we were cuddled together on his stiff, modular couch. "Has Nan opened up to you about any of this yet?"

I hadn't felt like catching him up on the phone, preferring instead to talk in person. Besides, I knew he'd be distracted until he was able to get away from the office. "Nothing. And according to Paisley, they spent that time away from home in a motel."

"A motel? But Nan has plenty of friends.

Why didn't she stay with one of them?" Charles hadn't known Nan that long, but even he understood how weird this all was.

I burrowed deeper into his arms, safe there even as the rest of my world crumbled around me. "I'm worried about her. She looked so different when she came home today. So empty. Whatever this secret is, it's weighing heavily on her. I'm honestly not sure whether she'll ever be ready to talk about it."

He rubbed reassuring little circles in my shoulder. "Are you okay with that?"

I closed my eyes and thought about it for the millionth time since Pringle handed me that old letter. No matter which way I looked at the situation, my answer always remained the same. "I wish I could be, but no. I need to know."

Charles nodded. "I understand. If it were me, I'd want to know, too." Thank goodness for understanding boyfriends. It wasn't just that he understood, either. He wanted to help.

Remembering our newest puzzle piece suddenly, I pulled the picture of Nan and

William from my purse and handed it to him. "The animals found this in her room today."

He held the old photograph between us, and we both stared down at the faces caught in time. "The mysterious William, I presume?"

I nodded. "Pringle and Octo-Cat found it in her room."

He chuckled softly and pressed a kiss to my temple. "Those two."

"Yeah." I smiled, but only a little.

Charles sat up straighter. "Those two," he said with more vigor this time. "They're quite the duo. Why don't you bring them here?"

I looked up at him with unblinking eyes, not quite understanding what he wanted—or why he'd invite the trouble-making raccoon into his abode.

He stood and pulled me to my feet with both hands. "Before I bought this house, it belonged to Nan, and for more than thirty years at that. What if there are still some old secrets hidden inside?"

The last little flickering bit of hope

burned brighter. "Charles, that's a great idea."

"Thank me later. Right now, let's get the rest of our search team and inform them of the plan."

We drove back to my place together and gathered the cat and raccoon for the journey. Octo-Cat was less than enthused, but Pringle whooped with joy to learn he'd be accompanying us on an off-property adventure—no stowing away required.

"This is where I grew up," I told him once we'd arrived.

He scrunched up his nose as if something smelled bad. "You and Charles grew up in the same house together? Isn't that a little…?"

When I explained this to my boyfriend, he laughed. "I live here now, but until a couple years ago I lived in California. That's where I grew up, and it's just about as far away as you can get and stay in the same country."

Octo-Cat patrolled the room; his nose also twitched in disgust. "I wish I could say I like what he's done with the place, but that would be a lie."

"What's he saying?" Charles asked me.

A wicked smile crept across my face. "That he wants to say hi to his old friends Jacques and Jillianne," I said, referencing Charles's two hairless cats. They'd been crucial to a previous murder investigation, which meant we had spent plenty of time in their company. Octo-Cat found them creepy and tiresome, though, especially since they only spoke in rhymes and riddles.

"That was uncalled for," my cat hissed, then slinked off to hide beneath the dining room table. Although he was still in clear view, I decided to leave him alone. As he'd pointed out earlier, it was hard to search without fingers and opposable thumbs. I didn't want to force him only for him to be frustrated and mopey the rest of the night. He'd help if he wanted to.

"Well, unless we can get the cats on board, that leaves three of us for the search," I summed up for Charles. "Are you ready, Pringle?"

He rubbed his hands together and

leaned forward. "Oh, yeah, baby. I'm off to find the attic. See you kids later."

We both watched him scamper away. "You do know there's a pretty good chance he'll steal from you, right?"

Charles shrugged. "Small price to pay if it helps."

"So where do we start?" I asked. Even though I'd grown up here, this was his place now and I worked hard to respect that.

"When I moved in, there were still a couple of boxes tucked away in the garage. I say we start there."

I nodded and followed him out of the house.

"How are you taking this all?" he asked once we had the boxes pulled out and opened in front of us.

"Not well," I admitted with a sigh, growing increasingly frustrated as I rummaged through the various gardening supplies that filled the boxes.

"This is hopeless," I whined and sunk to the garage floor in a crouch. "Nan kept this secret for almost fifty years. Why do I think I have any chance of solving it now?"

Charles bent over me and forced my chin up so that we could look into each other's eyes. "Because you're Angie freaking Russo, that's why. You're the smartest, the prettiest, the best, and you've got this."

My heart soared. "Charles, you're—wait!"

His eyes crinkled around the corners with curiosity as he studied me.

"Turn around and look up. Look there!" I cried and pointed toward the rafters above. There, a dusty old box sat tucked into the corner. The aged cardboard had faded to the color of the wooden planks that held it aloft, making it almost impossible to spot unless you knew what you were looking for. Well, I'd seen it, and something told me it held important information.

"I'll get the ladder," Charles said, popping to his feet. "You spot me while I climb."

With a bit of fancy maneuvering, we were able to hoist the box from its hiding place and wrestle it to the garage floor. Inside, we found the jackpot of memorabilia—an old letter jacket, school projects, a collection of homemade clay sculptures, and a photo album.

"Bingo," I said on the wings of a happy sigh, wasting no time before I began flipping through the pages. I recognized pictures of my great grandparents and of little Nan. Normally, seeing these new family memories would give me special warm fuzzies, but we were on a mission here.

"Wait, look there!" Charles cried, slamming his index finger on the page before I could turn it again. He'd pointed to a young man wearing a light-colored suit and standing before a church sign that proclaimed:

Easter Services
This Sunday
8 AM 10 AM 6 PM

"Look familiar?" Charles asked, lifting his finger and pointing again in excitement.

I strained harder as I eyed the picture,

finally noticing the dimples that lined either side of the man's smile. The rest fell into place shortly after that. "It's William McAllister."

"And look at the sign," he urged me.

When I read the service times aloud, he shook his head and pointed higher. "The name of the church, there." More pointing.

"Faith Baptist Church, Larkhaven, GA. Est. 1903," I read. "Do you think the church is still there? That they would have information on William or his heirs?"

Charles's smile widened. "There's only one way to find out."

CHAPTER EIGHTEEN

My hands shook as I punched in the number Charles and I had found on the church website. Sure enough, it was still standing, still serving the small community of Larkhaven, Georgia.

But would the people who worshipped there now remember my nan and her William from all those years ago?

Part of me hoped they would, but another huge part was afraid of what they might reveal. William's letter had hinted at trouble. Did I want to know if he and Nan had been engaged in some kind of nefarious doings? Or what if Nan was innocent in all this, but William had hurt her? What if she just wanted to forget, but I was forcing all those terrible memories to the surface?

Charles sat so close to me that our legs touched from hip to knee. "You can do this. Deep breaths."

"It's the moment of truth," Octo-Cat said sagely from across the room. He'd found a sunbeam filtering in from between the slatted blinds, and now he and Charles's Sphynx cats lay sunning themselves like tiny sea lions on a thin outcropping of rocks.

"Also, you can do this," Octo-Cat added with a supportive purr.

Pringle still hadn't returned from his investigation of the attic, but I had all the support I needed to take this next step. The only thing holding me back was my own fear.

And I'd faced down murderers before and lived to tell the tale. How could this be anywhere near that bad?

Just one little phone call…

I finished entering the number and put my cell phone on speaker.

"First Baptist of Larkhaven," a woman with a perky drawl answered. She seemed nice, like she'd want to help.

"Hello?" she repeated when I didn't immediately jump to explain myself.

"Oh, hi. My name's Angie, and I'm doing some research on my family. I was wondering if you might be able to help me?" I bit my lip and waited.

"I'm here for another few hours today. Would you like to stop in for a chat?" the woman said.

Charles squeezed my knee and mouthed, "You've got this."

I kept my eyes on him as I spoke to the lady on the other end of the line. "Actually, I live out of state and—well, it's kind of a complicated situation, but I was wondering if maybe you knew a man named William McAllister? He attended your church in the late sixties, and I think he's my long-lost grandpa."

"Oh, dear." She took a deep breath, and my heart sped to a nervous gallop. "That was before my time. Sad to say I never knew a William."

Another dead end. Shoot.

"Okay, thank you for your ti—"

Apparently, she wasn't done speaking yet, though.

"But the McAllisters still attend services every Sunday," the woman continued. "Would you like a phone number for them?"

Charles gave me a thumbs up and bobbed his head enthusiastically. He smiled wide, and I couldn't help but smile, too.

"Y-y-yes." I stumbled over the short word, one that should have been easy but was impossibly difficult. "Please."

"You've got it, sugar. Just a second." The friendly secretary returned a couple minutes later and rattled off a number.

Charles typed it into a note on his phone while she read.

"That's for a Miss Linda McAllister," the church receptionist continued. "She's the oldest of the bunch so the one who's most likely to remember your grandfather. Good luck!"

"Thank you. You've been incredibly helpful," I said as new tears began to form in the corners of my eyes.

We said our goodbyes, and I sat silently holding my phone and crying huge, relieved tears while Charles placed a supportive arm around my shoulders.

"Are you going to call her?" he asked.

"I don't know," I mumbled, biting my lip again. "I'd rather Nan tell me than me having to find out from somebody else."

"Maybe. But she's not making a peep," Pringle said, returning with an overloaded armful of booty from Charles's attic. "And don't you think you deserve to know the truth about your own life?"

"What's he saying?" Charles asked, eyeing the raccoon with trepidation.

"That we should call," I said simply. Leave it to Pringle to want to learn whatever secrets he could, even if it stirred up drama.

Charles nodded and looked back toward me. "And what does Octo-Cat think?"

My cat stretched in the sun, blinking slowly. "Octo-Cat thinks Angela is smart enough to make her own decisions." It was one of the nicest things he'd ever said to me.

"He says it's my decision," I translated with a smile.

"And so it is. What about Jacques and Jillianne? What do they say?" Charles asked next. I knew exactly what he was doing, and I loved him for it. He was giving me the time to make the decision for myself, proving that there was no wrong call here.

The two Sphynx cats, however, had been strangely quiet this whole time. Even now Octo-Cat spoke for them.

"This whole thing is already a riddle, so they don't have anything to add. They're kind of nice when they shut up, aren't they? Good nap buddies." He yawned and rolled onto his back.

I laughed. "They have no opinion, "I told Charles.

He laughed, too, and squeezed my hand. "And here I always assumed they were these great intellectuals."

"What do you think?" I asked, turning into him.

"This time I agree with the cat. Your cat. Only you know the right course of action." He pressed a kiss to my lips, and for a little while, I found myself lost in loving surrender.

"I can't believe he's copying my line, using my words to do… well, that," Octo-Cat said with a shudder. "Well, J and J. It's been swell," he said to the two hairless cats on his way out of the living room. "But that's my cue to go."

"Let me guess," Charles said with a laugh. "He thinks we're disgusting and doesn't want to be around us anymore."

"Yup, but at least he didn't call you UpChuck this time. That's real progress." I sighed happily. No matter what happened next, I'd still have Charles, Octo-Cat, my mom, dad, and even Nan. Nothing had to change. I could choose what to do with the information once I had it. This was still my life, and I could live it how I wanted.

Charles kissed the part in my hair, then rested his cheek on my head. His voice rumbled through me as he said, "Well, what will it be, Angie?"

I took a deep breath, sat up straight, and placed the one call I knew I needed to make to get my life back on track.

This was my decision, and I was ready to

deal with whatever consequences came with it.

Here goes nothing.

CHAPTER NINETEEN

Several hours later, I sat on my front porch with a fresh mug of tea warming my hands against the chilly night air. I leaned back against the side railing with both legs stretched out before me. Paisley sat snuggled in my lap while Octo-Cat lay snoozing at my side. Pringle had already absconded into his private apartment with the new treasures Charles had allowed him to steal from his attic, and my boyfriend had gone home so that I could have this moment to myself.

"Thanks for agreeing to talk with me," I said to the elderly woman who sat on the nearby rocking chair, holding a full cup of tea in her hands as well.

"Of course, dear," she answered with a far-off smile that seemed to take almost all the energy she had. "I should have spoken with you about this much earlier."

I turned the mug in my hands, searching for the right words to move this conversation forward. It seemed an apology was the best place to start. "I shouldn't have given you an ultimatum, but—"

"Say no more." Her voice was soft and reassuring. "I shouldn't have pushed you to that point. Thank you for giving me the chance to explain for myself first."

"Nan, you know that no matter what happened back then, it doesn't erase all the amazing years we've had together. It doesn't change the fact that you're the person I love most in this entire world. You're my best friend."

Octo-Cat stirred in his sleep, just enough to grumble a protest.

"Well, you and Octo-Cat," I amended with a chuckle.

"Show me what you found," she said without further delay. I knew this was hard for her, but I was so appreciative she was facing that discomfort to give me the answers I craved.

Instead of calling the number the church lady had given me, I'd decided to call my nan and come clean, to tell her I'd been searching for answers and may have found some but would much rather talk to her first if she was willing.

She'd asked for a few hours to gather her bearings but said we could talk that night. And now here we were.

"You've already seen the letter and birth certificate. Pringle took those back. But we also have these two pictures." I set my tea to the side and rose carefully, holding Paisley as I stood.

"Ahh, William," Nan said, memories sparkling in her light eyes. But did they spark joy? I couldn't quite tell.

"Who was he to you?" I asked, still so confused by all I knew, all I still didn't know.

She touched the photo of his face with trembling fingers. "He was my best friend growing up. We did everything together.

Almost like a brother and sister, until we hit puberty, and then suddenly our relationship felt very different."

"You fell in love," I finished for her.

"I did," she admitted with a sad shake of her head. "And for a while I thought he loved me, too, but then Marilyn Jones came along."

"The name on the birth certificate." I remembered that first night standing out here by myself as I read the shocking contents of his letter, saw my mom's real birth certificate for the first time.

She nodded. "Your real nan."

"I don't understand. What happened?" I placed a comforting hand on her shoulder, urging her on. There was still so much more that hadn't been said.

"I don't know what happened to Marilyn, only that William said she was gone, and he was going back to war. He was worried about his daughter, about Laura, your mother. And he was right to worry, because he died in battle later that year."

Tears pricked at my eyes for the friend Nan had lost, for the grandfather I'd never gotten the chance to know. "Oh, Nan, I'm so sorry."

She sniffed and smiled up at me. "By then, I'd met and fallen for your grandfather. We legally adopted your mother and raised her as our own, always fearing that Marilyn would come calling and take our daughter away. For years, we looked over our shoulders. Not hiding, since I was in the public spotlight given my choice of work, but always watching."

"And then what happened?"

She shook hard, and I knew that we'd reached the hardest part of the story. This was the part of the memory she'd tried so hard to forget.

"When your mother was eleven, Marilyn found us. She came to one of my shows and confronted me after. Said William's sister had told her what he'd done and that she wanted her baby back." Tears splashed into her tea, but she wasn't drinking it, anyway.

I wanted to comfort her, but I couldn't move. What had almost happened? How different would my mom's life be if…? And would I have even been born?

"Oh my gosh, all those years later? What did you do?" I couldn't stand another moment not knowing.

"I agreed to meet her the next day, to bring Laura." Her voice cracked here. "And then your grandfather and I packed up and left town."

"To Blueberry Bay," I whispered.

"To Blueberry Bay," she confirmed.

"What happened to Marilyn?"

Nan shook her head vigorously. Her tea sloshed over the edges of her cup, but she didn't react. "I don't know. We walked away from everything so that we could keep our family together. Your mother hadn't been born to us, but she was ours. And I didn't know why William sent his only daughter away, but I knew him and knew he must have had his reasons."

"Wow." I breathed heavily, still in shock. "Does Mom know about all this?"

"Of course not." Nan's voice faltered in a rare show of fragility. "How can I tell her that I stole her?"

And just like that my legs worked again. I pulled my nan to her feet and hugged her tight. "You didn't know. Your best friend gave her to you, and you trusted him."

"Back then, yes," she whispered into my hair. "But I made a choice when Marilyn found us in New York. A selfish one that's kept Laura from knowing her real mother and you from knowing your real nan."

"You're my real nan," I said, wrapping my arms around her even tighter. "I told you nothing can change that. Not even this."

"I appreciate that, dear." She pulled back and studied me with a small smile and bright eyes. "Sometimes I think I let myself fall even in more in love with you than I allowed myself to love your mother, because I knew no one would show up and try to take you away."

This explained so much, why she had been the main one to raise me even though my parents were here and capable. Whatever the reasons for it, I'd loved my childhood and I loved my life. I loved the woman who had risked so much to give it to me.

I kissed her on the cheek. "I've loved every single day with you, Nan. Well, every day except for the one you took Paisley to a motel and hid from me."

We smiled at each other, then laughed together for what felt like the first time in ages.

"You don't hate me?" she asked with a squeak.

"I could never hate you." I paused before saying the next part in case it hurt her. "But I do want to meet her."

Nan nodded. "I figured you might."

"Where do we start?" I needed to know more, but I also needed us to do this side by side.

"Together." She reached out her hand and grasped mine. "I've spent so many years running from the truth. Now let's walk toward it together."

CHAPTER TWENTY

A lot happened rather quickly after that.

Nan showed me all the old photos and mementos she'd kept hidden for fear of exposing her secret history growing up in Georgia and falling in unrequited love with her best friend. I still didn't know why William had decided to entrust his baby to Nan when her mother was still very much alive. I think the only person who might know the answer to that was Ms. Marilyn Jones herself, but we had no idea where to start looking for her—or even if she was still alive all these years later.

Pringle took full credit for solving the case and decided his fee should be doubled for just how fast "he" had managed to solve the mystery. He also demanded that his payment be delivered within three days or it would need to be doubled again.

That payment? A new home, since we had irreparably damaged his under-porch apartment with our shovels. And because he had decided to ask for double, he also demanded that we erect a new office headquarters for Pringle Whisperer, P.I.

Luckily, we knew the very best handyman in all of Blueberry Bay, a certain Mr. Brock "Cal" Calhoun. Not only did he do fast, quality work, but he also didn't ask too many questions—like why a single woman and her grandmother needed not one, but two, tree forts erected in their backyard or why one of those forts also needed to be outfitted with electricity and a satellite TV dish.

Once Cal had finished building the twin tree forts and Pringle was all moved in, I introduced him to reality TV, the ultimate source of juicy secrets and real human drama—at least that's what I told him.

Sure enough, he immediately got sucked in to one of the longest running reality competitions of them all, which meant there were plenty of back episodes for him to watch. He enjoyed laughing at the humans and their weak skills when it came to surviving in the wild.

"Survivor!" he quipped somewhere into his umpteenth hour of viewing. "Ha! Put a raccoon in there with them, then you'll see what a real survivor looks like!"

Pringle had already begun to spend all his time in front of his new TV, which thankfully meant he stayed out of trouble. Well, at least for now.

Brilliantly, Octo-Cat had a fairly easy time convincing the raccoon to join our investigation firm rather than continuing to compete with us.

"Think about it, Pringle," my cat crooned. "You like secrets. Now your whole job is keeping track of our secrets. In fact, that's your new job title—Pringle, MSK. Master Secret Keeper."

"Oooh, that's even better than P.I.," he crowed. "It's got more letters. Better letters!"

Really, all that happened was that we moved our filing cabinets into his rarely used work fort, but at least I knew they were safe there, given the ferocity he used to protect all his favorite treasures.

When Cal had finished building the tree forts, he also fixed the hole in our roof so that no other animals would be able to crawl into our attic. He helped us clear out the space under our porch, too, and then laid down a solid stone base—also to keep the wildlife out. I didn't mind getting up close and personal with my animal neighbors, but we needed to have at least some boundaries.

Julie, for her part, was incredibly relieved to find that all the missing mail had been accounted for. Her bosses at the post office let her off the hook but made sure to promptly deliver flyers throughout town, warning of highly intelligent and very disturbed forest animals.

Honestly, it made me laugh.

Pringle, too.

When I brought one home to show him,

he grabbed it from my hands in delight and then raced around the neighborhood collecting as many as he could for his treasure trove. I had no doubt that he'd eventually turn them all into sloppily constructed origami cranes, provided he stopped watching TV long enough to get to work.

While all this was great, the most important follow-up item still remained. Nan and I needed to reunite the family.

That's why my mom was here with us now.

Nan had baked all her favorites and encouraged her to dig in while she shared pictures and explained our shared, but until now hidden, past. Pringle had even generously returned the birth certificate and William's letter to us, so we could show them to her as a way of starting the conversation.

"There's still a lot we don't know," I explained to my mom, who sat stoically, taking it all in. I guess since she was an investigative reporter, she was used to larger-than-life stories like this one. It still couldn't have made any of this easier.

"I can't believe it. I have another mother out there," Mom said with a genuine smile. "What was she like?"

"I didn't really know her," Nan explained. "But she was beautiful, just like you." She bumped my arm. "And you, dear."

"Can we find her? Can I meet her?" Mom asked with a determined glint in her eyes. She never backed away from a challenge, and that proved true now, too.

"I'm not giving up until we do," I promised, taking my mom's hand and giving it a tight squeeze. "But we have even more family out there, family we haven't gotten the chance to know yet."

Nan sucked in a shaky breath, and I offered her a reassuring smile before turning back to my mom and revealing, "I have their phone number. Should we call?"

We caught Mom up on the McAllisters of Larkhaven, Georgia, and the help I'd received from the church receptionist.

"Can we really call them?" Mom asked. "Just like that?"

"Hey, you never know," I said with a goofy smile. "Maybe they've been looking for us, too."

"There's only one way to find out," Nan said, hugging us both from behind.

"Are you really okay with this?" Mom asked. "It must be so scary for you to go back to that time, that place."

"I'm not going back," Nan said with a wistful smile. "Only forward with my two girls."

Mom nodded, and I punched in the number I'd long since memorized even though this was the first time I was actually placing a call.

It rang three times, and then…

"Hello?" a woman who sounded about Mom's age answered.

"Is this Linda McAllister?" I asked through happy tears. I already knew what the answer to my question would be. "Because I think we might be related."

Even though she hadn't expected our call, we spent over two hours chatting about our lives, growing closer and closer, until there was no doubt in any of our minds that we were, in fact, family.

"So, when are you coming down to Larkhaven to see me?" Linda asked.

"Soon," I answered with an enormous smile. "Real soon."

WHAT'S NEXT?

Ever feel like your entire world has been turned on its head? That's how I've felt ever since the gang and I found out that Nan has been keeping major family secrets stashed neatly away in the attic.

What's worse, she won't stop talking about them now that they're out in the open. I still have so many questions, though. Like is she still the same woman I always assumed she was? And can I ever fully trust her again?

When Nan refuses to give me a straight answer, I invite my parents to join me for a cross-country train trip so that we can all discover the truth, once and for all.

WHAT'S NEXT?

Octo-Cat hitches a ride with us, too, and it's a good thing he does, because it isn't long before a dead body joins us in the dining car. Now we have two mysteries to solve, and fast—our lives and legacy depend on it.

Pre-order to save! HIMALAYAN HAZARD is just $2.99 until it releases on November 14.

Get your copy here!
mollymysteries.com/HimalayanH

SNEAK PEEK: RACCOON RACKETEER

My name's Angie Russo, and lately my life has taken one dramatic turn after another. Seriously, where can I even begin?

I guess it all starts with my cat.

Think that sounds boring? Well, think again!

My cat can talk. Only to me, but still.

We met at the law firm where I used to work as a paralegal. I never really loved that job, but I did enjoy having food in my fridge and a roof over my head, so I stayed despite being treated like a glorified secretary and not the shrewd researcher I'd worked so hard to become.

We had a will reading scheduled one

morning, and I was called in to make some coffee for the attendees. The machine we had was approximately a million years old and unpredictable even on its best day. This was not one of its best days. All I wanted to do was make the cruddy coffee and get back to work, but—lo and behold—I got electrocuted and knocked unconscious instead.

And when I awoke from that zap, I found a striped cat sitting on my chest and making some pretty mean jokes at my expense. Well, as soon as I realized the voice was coming from him and he realized that I could understand what he said, that cat recruited me to help solve the murder of his late owner.

That's how I and Octavius Maxwell Ricardo Edmund Frederick Fulton Russo, Esq., P.I. became an item. I've since shortened his name to Octo-Cat and have become his official owner—although he'd surely tell you that he's the one who owns me, and, well… he wouldn't exactly be wrong.

He came into my life first with a murder mystery and then with a generous trust fund and even more generous list of demands. So now here we are, living in the posh manor house that previously belonged to his late owner, drinking chilled Evian out of Lenox teacups, and operating the area's best—and only—private investigation firm.

There was a brief upset when a raccoon named Pringle set up a competing business, but we've moved past that now. Because, yeah, at first I could only talk to Octo-Cat, but with time, I also gained the ability to communicate with other animals, too.

The regular cast of mammalian characters that make up my life include an eternally optimistic rescue Chihuahua named Paisley, that infamous raccoon racketeer named Pringle—also known as the Master Secret Keeper for our firm—an easily distracted, nut-obsessed squirrel named Maple, and my crazy-daisy, live-in grandmother, Nan.

Frankly, I'd love to add a bird to our merry little gang of forest misfits, but they're all too frightened to talk to either me or Octo-Cat. Go figure.

And despite our diverse skill set, our P.I.

outfit isn't exactly successful. We've only had one case to date, and we weren't even paid for it. I know it will happen for us eventually if we just stay the course and continue to believe in ourselves…

Um, right?

Well, that's what Paisley insists, anyway.

Even still, I've got this huge new thing in my life that is keeping us plenty busy, with or without work to fill our days. I just discovered that I have a whole big family in Larkhaven, Georgia, that I never even knew existed until a couple weeks ago. And what's more, they've invited me, my mom, and dad to come down for an extended visit so that we can all get to know each other.

Octo-Cat insists on coming, too. He hates long car rides and refuses to even consider getting on a plane, which means we get to take the train. Whoopee.

Sure, it won't cost very much, but it will take longer than a day of continuous travel to get there. Still, I can't exactly leave him behind when he was a big part of helping me locate the hidden branch of our family.

Yeah, Nan had kept them hidden from

us for my entire life and my mom's whole life, too. But now that we've found them again, there's no keeping us apart. Nan doesn't want to join us, even though Mom and I both assured her she'd be welcome. She still feels guilty about what happened.

Maybe we can convince her to join us for the next visit. I hope we can, because even though she kept a major secret from me, she's still my best friend and my very favorite person in the whole wide world.

That's why saying goodbye to her right now is so difficult…

"Promise me you'll call every single day," I moaned, hugging my grandmother so tight I had to wonder if she could even breathe.

"Mommy, I'm going to miss you, too!" Paisley, Nan's five-pound tricolor Chihuahua, cried as she pranced on the platform from the other end of her neon pink leash.

I scooped her up and peppered her adorable little face with kisses. "I'm going to miss you, too," I cooed in a cutesy, crazy pet lady voice. Talking to the animals like this in public made people think I was weird but kept my secret ability hidden. "Mommy will be back in sixteen days. You can wait sixteen days, can't you?"

"I don't know how to count," Paisley said with a happy bark.

I handed her over to Nan and took Octo-Cat's cat carrier from my mom so she could get in goodbye hugs, too.

My cat growled during the handoff. "Hey, there's delicate cargo in here!"

Mom and Nan said a quick goodbye, and then I set Octo-Cat down to hug her again. As pathetic as it might be to admit, I'd never been away from her so long. I'd grown up under her roof and lived with her most of my adult life, too—although now she lived with me rather than the other way around.

Throngs of passengers dragging big wheeled suitcases passed us on either side, and I had to step to the side to avoid getting hit by a fast-walking woman who was more focused on her phone conversation than where she was going.

"Look," I told Octo-Cat. "She has a cat carrier, too."

And she did. Only it was much fancier. I wouldn't be surprised if the bling adorning the case was actual diamonds—or at least Swarovski crystals.

"Show-off," my cat muttered, even though I'm pretty sure he'd have loved a decked-out carrier like that to call his own. It didn't matter that he'd sooner surrender one of his few remaining lives than willingly get inside.

"I'm surprised there are so many people out here," my dad said, glancing around uncomfortably. "I didn't realize anyone still took trains when there are so many other options available."

"It's romantic," my mom gushed, leaning into him and possibly squeezing his butt from behind. It seriously grossed me out how in love these two were, even after thirty years of marriage. They sure acted like high schoolers, sometimes.

"I feel like I'm about to rush platform

nine and three quarters at Kings Cross for the first time," I said with a snort and a chuckle.

"When were you at Kings Cross?" my dad asked with a furrowed brow.

Ah, jeez. Sometimes it was hard being the only avid reader in the family. Had my parents seriously not even seen the movies?

"That's it!" I cried. "We've got like thirty hours aboard that train. More than enough time for a Harry Potter movie marathon, and when we get home, I'm lending you my book collection so that we can get you all the way caught up."

"Homework?" my mom whined.

"Ugh, you're the worst ever, Mom," my dad added.

And then they kissed so long and hard that my mom's foot popped up like a fairy-tale princess getting her first big kiss. Only this was their six millionth big kiss at least.

This was going to be a very long trip. Very long, indeed.

"The conductor's waving you over," Nan said, pointing toward a uniformed man standing just outside of our train car. "Best get a move on."

"Are you ready?" I asked Octo-Cat.

"Just get me out of this thing," he grumbled, as if this whole method of travel hadn't been his idea.

"Relax," I murmured as we made our way over to the step up into the train. "I'll have you out in two minutes, and then it will be smooth sailing from there. After all, what's the worst thing that can happen on a train?"

Famous last words… I really should have known better.

Pre-order to save! HIMALAYAN HAZARD is just $2.99 until it releases on November 14.

Get your copy here!
mollymysteries.com/HimalayanH

WHAT'S AFTER THAT?

Nobody does the holidays like small-town Maine, and my particular small town just so happens to be the very best at decking the halls and rocking around the big Christmas tree downtown.

Yes, every year, Glendale puts on a Holiday Spectacular that's grander and greater than the one that came before. Unfortunately, the only thing everyone's going to remember this year is the two dead bodies that show up in the center of the ice sculpture garden.

With the whole town having come out to play, everyone's in close proximity to the crime scene—and everyone's a suspect. A great many fingers are pointed my way, too, since it was me and my cat who discovered the deathly duo. With only my whacky Nan, overly optimistic Chihuahua, and snarky feline to help me, can I clear my name and save Christmas all in one perfectly executed investigation?

Hold on to your jingle bells, because it's going to be a wild ride.

Pre-order to save! HOPPY HOLIDAY HOMICIDE is just $2.99 until it releases on December 12.

Get your copy here! mollymysteries.com/HoppyHolidayH

MORE FROM BLUEBERRY BAY

Welcome to Blueberry Bay, a scenic region of Maine peppered with quaint small towns and home to a shocking number of mysteries. If you loved this book, then make sure to check out its sister series from other talented Cozy Mystery authors…

Pet Whisperer P.I.
By Molly Fitz

Glendale is home to Blueberry Bay's first ever talking cat detective. Along with his ragtag gang of human and animal helpers, Octo-Cat is determined to save the day… so long as it doesn't interfere with his schedule. Start with book one, *Kitty Confidential*, which is now available to buy or borrow! Visit Visit www.QuirkyCozy.com/PetWhisperer for more.

Little Dog Diner
By Emmie Lyn

Misty Harbor boasts the best lobster rolls in all of Blueberry Bay. There's another thing that's always on the menu, too. Murder! Dani and her little terrier, Pip, have a knack for being in the wrong place at the wrong time… which often lands them smack in the middle of a fresh, new murder mystery and in the crosshairs of one cunning criminal after the next. Start with book one, *Mixing Up Murder*, which is now available to buy or borrow! Visit www.QuirkyCozy.com/LittleDog for more.

Shelf Indulgence
By S.E. Babin

Dewdrop Springs is home to Tattered Pages, a popular bookshop with an internet cafe, a grumpy Persian cat named Poppy, and some of the most suspicious characters you'll ever meet. And poor Dakota Adair has just inherited it all. She'll need to make peace with her new cat and use all her book smarts to catch a killer or she might be the next to wind up dead in the stacks. Book one, *Hardback Homicide*, will be coming soon. Keep an eye on www.QuirkyCozy.com for more.

Haunted Housekeeping
By R.A. Muth

Cooper's Cove is home to Blueberry Bay's premier estate cleaning service. Tori and Hazel, the ill-fated proprietors of

Bubbles and Troubles, are prepared to uncover a few skeletons. But when a real one turns up, they'll have to solve the mystery quickly if they're going to save their reputations—and their lives. Book one, *The Squeaky Clean Skeleton*, will be coming soon. Keep an eye on www.QuirkyCozy.com for more.

The Kindergarten Coven
By F.M. Storm

Quiet, secluded, and most importantly, far away from his annoying magical family, Guy couldn't wait to start a new life on Caraway Island. Unfortunately, he hadn't counted on his four-year-old daughter coming into her own witchy powers early… or on her accidentally murdering one of the PTO moms. Oops! Book one, *Stay-at-Home Sorcery*, will be coming soon. Keep an eye on www.QuirkyCozy.com for more.

ABOUT MOLLY FITZ

While USA Today bestselling author Molly Fitz can't technically talk to animals, she and her doggie best friend, Sky Princess, have deep and very animated conversations as they navigate their days. Add to that, five more dogs, a snarky feline, comedian husband, and diva daughter, and you can pretty much imagine how life looks at the Casa de Fitz.

Molly lives in a house on a high hill in the Michigan woods and occasionally ventures out for good food, great coffee, or to meet new animal friends.

Writing her quirky, cozy animal mysteries is pretty much a dream come true, but she also goes by the name Melissa Storm (also a USA Today bestselling author, yay!) and writes a very different kind of story.

Learn more, grab the free app, or sign up for her newsletter at www.MollyMysteries.com!

MORE FROM MOLLY

If you're ready to dive right in to more Pet Whisperer P.I., then you can even order the other books right now by clicking below:

[Kitty Confidential](#)

[Terrier Transgressions](#)

[Hairless Harassment](#)

[Dog-Eared Delinquent](#)

[The Cat Caper](#)

[Chihuahua Conspiracy](#)

[Raccoon Racketeer](#)

[Himalayan Hazard](#)

[Hoppy Holiday Homicide](#)

[Retriever Ransom](#)

Lawless Litter

Legal Seagull

Pet Whisperer P.I. Books 1-3

Six Merry Little Murders

CONNECT WITH MOLLY

Sign up for Molly's newsletter for book updates and cat pics:
mollymysteries.com/subscribe

Download Molly's app for cool bonus content:
mollymysteries.com/app

Join Molly's reader group on Facebook to make new friends: **mollymysteries.com/group**

Made in the USA
Las Vegas, NV
21 April 2021